Two Weeks

This is a work of fiction. Names, characters, and incidents are either the product of the author's imagination or used fictitiously. Several actual historical persons are used however, there is no evidence that any such incidents as described in this novel ever occurred. Any other resemblances to actual persons, either living or dead, business establishments, events or locales is entirely coincidental.

Cover Design by Renne Rhae
www. rrhaestudios.com

Visit www.booksurge.com to order additional copies

Also available on Amazon.com

Two Weeks

A Short Novel

by

W. H. Short

2007

Dedication
To My Mother
Margaret Dolores Short
(1928-2007)
She always believed in me

Acknowledgments

Thanks so much to the many family members who first read the drafts of this manuscript and provided input: Lorraine, Arlene, D.D., Freda, Marla, Dave, Scott, and my Mom. No one who writes in a family does so without affecting everyone. They all tolerated my madness.

Thanks to Tamara Knabb for the serious editing that needed to be done.

Thanks to Renne Rhae for the book cover design.

Thanks to John and Marsha Perkins and the King Author Court association for their support.

One last thanks to all of the fine Marines I have had the pleasure of knowing and serving with.

Prologue

1993

When Judge Pamela Marks-Campbell walked in the front door and into her living room, she found her son, Jack, sitting in a chair. She was startled to see him there. What a pleasant surprise! He looked so handsome in his marine uniform with the shiny gold bars of a second lieutenant. It still amazed her. There had never been even a hint when he was growing up that he might become a marine. Could it be that he was just a chip off the old block? Oh, how serious he looked. Was it just military bearing, or was there something else?

"Dear, so happy to see you," she chirped gleefully. His visits came so infrequently, especially now that he was a marine. "How long can you stay? Will you be staying for dinner?"

Jack stood and turned his head automatically to one side so his mother could give him her standard welcome kiss on the side of his cheek. It was somewhat of a formality between the two, but after years of training, he knew what she wanted. He was more than a head taller than she was, and she had to stand on her toes, even in heels, to perform the ritual.

"I will stay for dinner," he replied as a matter of fact. "We have something important to discuss."

Waves of emotions flooded through her. She was proud of the man he had become. She could sense that he had a specific purpose for this visit, and now she was curious.

"Fine, it will only take me a few minutes. Tonight is Mary's night off, but she always leaves something in the fridge for a quick warm up. Let's change into something more comfortable, and I'll heat up dinner."

Jack just nodded his head. He followed her up the stairs, and when they reached the top, he went toward his old room. He had not lived in it for over five years, but he knew there would be a change of clothes there. She had not disturbed his room since he had left for college. The poster of Loni Anderson was still on the back of the door. He found a pair of jeans and a sweatshirt in the dresser. He noticed that something had changed; his old jeans were loose on his waist. Jack left his uniform folded in a precision military manner on the bed.

Meanwhile, Pam had changed into slacks and a summer blouse and had already started dinner. Jack went into the kitchen, sat at the bar, and just watched his mother. He looked at her carefully for the first time in years. He knew she was in her mid-forties, forty-five, he thought. She had always been slim, and she still had an attractive figure. Her hair was flaming red, and she had the freckles to go with it. It was her eyes he always remembered, those piercing green eyes that seemed to look right through him, especially when she imposed her Scottish will on him. His mother had always been the strength of the family.

She put the salad on the bar and fixed their plates while he set the table. They had old routines from years before, but when they started eating, he just sat there silently picking at his food. She could see in his face that he was a million miles away.

After a while she spoke, "Well, dear, what's so important?"

"You know that Dad has been sick again?" He started.

"No. I'm sorry I was not aware." She responded.

Pam had been divorced from Charley for almost eighteen years. She hadn't spoken to him more than a half dozen times in the past ten years, and it had been more than three years since she'd last seen him. They had no financial ties anymore, and she suspected that she made more money than he did. Their only link was their children, and now, with both Jack and Sarah grown, there was nothing left for them to talk about.

"Dad's not actually why I'm here. I came to ask you about my real father."

Pam gasped! She hadn't expected this. She fought to control her face. He knew! But, how? Her reaction had confirmed his suspicions.

"What makes you think that Charley is not your father?" she asked guardedly.

"I was asked by his doctors to test as a possible kidney donor for him. Sarah was tested at the same time. She is a perfect match, and is going to be the donor. I was taken aside and they explained to me that I was not even a close match. In fact, my blood type and his are totally incompatible. There is no possibility that he can be my father."

Well, there it was, after all these years! She supposed that she had always known this day would come.

"Have you discussed this with Charley?"

"No," he replied. Suddenly a new thought occurred to him. "You mean, he doesn't know?"

"Of course he knows." She leaned forward and looked Jack directly in the eyes. "And now that you know, there are a total of three people who know. I would prefer that Grandma never knows."

"Okay," he hesitated, and then persisted, "but, you are going to tell me about my real father aren't you?"

She got up and walked out, nodding yes. Jack sat there feeling numb. He had not wanted to hurt his mother, but since he had found out that Charley was not his real father, his whole world had crumbled. What else didn't he know? Was anything in his life real? At first he had been angry with his mother, but he could not stay angry. She had always been so supportive of his choices, even when he had decided to join the marines. He had thought she would be upset, but she hadn't been. In fact, he was surprised to discover that she knew a lot about the Marine Corps. He still felt somewhat betrayed, but now he just wanted an explanation from her.

Jack looked around him as he waited. Nothing changed. He sat at the same dining table where he'd eaten so many meals while growing up. The room opened out into a living room where the same couch and coffee table sat before the fireplace. Tall bookcases filled with beautiful editions stood on either side of the mantle. His mother never rearranged furniture. Even the curtains were the same. His mother had good taste, and this was a grand room.

Jack looked up as his mother walked back into the room carrying a box. It was old and frayed, taped back together on several different occasions. She opened it carefully and removed a faded green book. Jack had seen hundreds of such books. It was a standard U. S. government green-book used by marines to keep logs and journals. She hugged it to her chest. Tears formed in the corners of her eyes.

"I cannot tell you about him, Jack, but you can read about him." She held out the book with both hands. As Jack stood and gently took it from her hands, she continued, "I wrote this before you were born. When I started writing, I did not even know that I was pregnant. No one has ever read it. Maybe I should have told you the truth before now." Jack started to speak, but she quickly held up her hand. "No more questions, Jack. Just read the book."

Jack held the book like a piece of live ordnance. The binding creaked as he opened it; the pages were yellowed with age. His mother had always had beautiful handwriting. When he looked up she was gone. So, he sat back down and started reading.

March 1968

I find myself compelled to write this narrative about the most eventful two weeks of my short life to date. I feel that for the first time I've lived; truly lived. I believe I now have a better understanding of life, love, beauty, and the real meaning of freedom. I've taken many classes where words have been used to attempt to explain these concepts. I now believe that these things can only be thoroughly understood and appreciated by living on the edge with the meaning of these noble concepts.

I am riding on a bus going back to college. It's a place that will never be the same for me. I'm setting new life goals for myself. Never before, even as a young girl, have I felt the need to keep a diary or personal notes. But, the events of just two short weeks have changed everything. I am awash in new emotions, and I feel more alive than I ever have in my life. I am happy, but I am also sad. I'm so angry with him, and yet so in love. I admit to being totally confused. Maybe by writing everything down, I can make some sense of it all. So, here goes. I must start at the beginning:

Day 1

It's hard to believe that only two weeks have passed since I left campus on the bus. We spent the first day on the bus driving from campus to Washington. I was so proud and excited just to be invited to go. We were on our way to Washington DC; I had never been and was so excited I could barely contain my trembling. This was an important political trip for all of us. We felt that our nation's elected officials had lost touch with what the public wants and believes, that they didn't understand the new age we are entering; or so I thought at the time. We were on our way to picket the White House to protest the war in Vietnam.

We sang protest songs all night long as the bus rolled along. The pungent smell of pot permeated the air as some of the kids passed a joint around. We were so happy, carefree, and naïve, yet we were on a serious mission. We'd been told that if enough of us would protest, maybe some of the lives being wasted in the war could be saved.

Day 2 - Morning

I was tired when we arrived in the early morning dawn. Nevertheless, I was awake and looking at the famous monuments when the bus rolled into the city. Traffic was light as we'd beaten the morning traffic rush. The only reservation I had about the trip came from the argument I'd had with Daddy. I had called home before leaving campus and had talked with both Mother and Daddy about my plans. Mother, as usual, understood without really understanding. No matter what, she always went along with anything I did. Daddy, however, was a problem. When I explained to him that I was going to Washington D.C. to protest, he blew a gasket.

"I'm not spending five thousand dollars a semester for you to run off to Washington to hoot and holler at the politicians. No matter what you do, it will not change anything!" he had raged.

"But Daddy," I explained, "It's during break, and we'll be back when classes start in two weeks. This is just so important! I will be part of history."

"You are only nineteen years old, and any young girl can get into a lot of trouble in a town like that. There are no proper chaperones, and you say you're not even staying in a hotel! How safe can that be?" Then he said, "I forbid it!"

I got angry; why couldn't he just accept that I was no longer a child? I told him coldly, "I am going Daddy, and there is nothing you can do about it!" I slammed the receiver down so hard I hurt my hand.

When we arrived in Washington it was cold, and a new snow had just begun sprinkling the ground, but it was not going to stick. The wind was so cold it cut right through me.

I was assigned to the White House picket. We used signs that another group had passed down to us from the day before. I learned that new signs were only made when the old ones wore out. The signs were passed out to us randomly and the one I got read: 'STOP THE WAR! – STOP KILLING BABIES!' It had the peace symbol in each corner.

Our leader, Professor Bruce Norton, gave a little speech. He explained that the war-protest movement is only the beginning of a larger, more important movement against the establishment. Not only was war evil, but the capitalist pigs that controlled everything had to be stopped. According to Bruce, capitalists ruled the politicians and the workers of America; and only when they were defeated could there be true freedom in America.

That confused me. Daddy owns a large company employing hundreds of people. I was mad at Daddy, but he was not evil. He worried about the people working for him. On several occasions he had talked about what would happen if his company didn't get certain contracts. I'd never heard Daddy say it would hurt profits; he worried that jobs would be lost and his employees would be hurt. These were the things I thought about as we walked along the fence on Pennsylvania Avenue. When we arrived in front of the White House, we started walking in a long circle, trying to stay out of the street. There was a lot of traffic on Pennsylvania Avenue, and it would not do to get run down.

I guess I should explain about the set up. Our bus was parked on a street by the National Mall, which was much bigger than I'd expected. The Mall is a vast, mostly grassy area that stretches over a mile from the Lincoln Memorial at one end, to the Capitol building at the other. The Washington Memorial and the famous Reflecting Pool sit between them. Only seeing the Mall with my own eyes could allow me to fully appreciate the breathtaking beauty of it.

I had heard that there were tours of the White House, and I was wondering if we would get a chance to take one. When I mentioned that to my friend, Betty, she was amazed that I would even consider such a thing. I wouldn't chance mentioning my curious desires again.

The news people showed up at about ten o'clock in the morning with their cameras. They walked around and filmed the picket line for a few minutes. One of the reporters spoke briefly with Bruce, and then they were gone. I was told this was normal. There was another group of protesters at the steps of the Capitol, and between the two groups we were good for at least five minutes on the evening newscast on TV. That was about all the time we'd get unless the cops showed up and started beating on one of the protesters. It wasn't all that long ago that the evening news was only fifteen minutes long, but between the war and civil rights protesters, they now had enough news to make it last half an hour.

Day 2 - Evening

As the afternoon wore on, it got colder. The snow had stopped, but the temperature continued to drop. We had our warm clothes from school with us, but they were just for walking from one building to another between classes. I know I'm a girl from Illinois, and I go to school in Wisconsin, but I got cold! I wasn't the only one, either. Maybe I just wasn't used to being outdoors all day long, and as the day wore on I got even colder. One of the older students, Tom, had a thermos filled with brandy, and after a while, we were all drinking brandy. By three o'clock in the afternoon my feet and hands were numb, and the colder it got, the more I drank. We quit picketing just as it was getting dark.

The walk back across the Mall was difficult. I thought I would never make it. It really was not that far, but between the brandy and the cold it seemed like an eternity of misery. When I got back to the bus it was obvious that the other girls were just as cold as I was. Tom started the bus and got the heater going. Meanwhile, some of the kids had unpacked tents and campfire stoves. I huddled inside the bus trying to get warm. Someone placed a cup of coffee laced with whisky in my hands. It was warm, so I gulped it down. After about an hour of sitting by the heater and drinking four more doctored coffees, I finally started to warm up. But the truth is that by this time I could feel no pain, or cold.

Then I realized I'd forgotten something that I wished I'd thought of earlier. I went to the back of the bus and found my sleeping bag, unzipped it, and wrapped it around me. Finally, some real warmth! I suddenly realized that I had not eaten all day. I had money, but lacked the strength to walk to a restaurant, so I went outside and joined the others sitting around a big Coleman heater. Betty gave me a sandwich, which I consumed immediately. That was followed by yet another new drink: hot buttered rum.

In spite of my alcohol-induced haze at the time, I can still remember some of the talk around the heater. It was strictly politics: Would President Johnson seek another term? Certainly no Democrat could oppose the president. Who did Nixon think he was? Wasn't he the guy who lost to John Kennedy and couldn't even get elected as governor in California? But most of the talk was about the war, and whether there would be another offensive in the spring like there had been in the past couple of years. But what agitated most of the guys was the draft. Some of the guys were seriously talking about going to Canada rather than going into the army. Some said that they could not fight a war that was immoral and oppressive to the innocent. It certainly seemed to make sense at the time; why fight another country's war? No one in Vietnam was going to invade the United States, so why fight the war?

Sometime between seven and eight o'clock, I fell asleep listening to all the talk. Actually, as much as I had to drink, I probably passed out. When I woke several hours later I was not alone in my sleeping bag; Bruce was with me, and he had his hands all over me. He had carried me under the bus, and we were alone. I was a little scared, but he was our authority figure, so I was reluctant to cry out and seem childish. In retrospect, I probably should have started screaming.

Bruce was kissing me and running his hands over my skin and through my hair. Before this I had thought I kind of liked him, but I wasn't so sure anymore. This was definitely not a good situation. I was still somewhat groggy, and as he continued to grope me I became more and more frightened. He pushed my bra up above my breasts and continued groping me.

"Please don't!" I protested.

"Come on baby, this is what it's all about," he told me as

he pulled me even closer to him. "Free love."

"No, Bruce. Stop. I don't feel like it! Stop!" I realized he wasn't going to listen to me and I began to panic. He ran his hand up my leg; it was only then that I realized that while I had been unconscious, he had removed my long johns and panties. I was completely vulnerable. I started to yell and thrash, trying to get out of the sleeping bag. I vaguely remember hitting my head on the underside of the bus, yet I somehow managed to get free and crawl out from beneath the bus. Bruce was saying something, but I couldn't understand him.

I ran, and he chased me. I crossed the street and went up the first alley I came to. I ran hard, and all the way I could hear his footsteps behind me. As I rounded the corner I ran headlong into a young man. He held on to me to keep me from falling. I was gasping so hard from running that I couldn't even speak. I must have looked a sight, covered with sweat and some blood from where I'd hit my head on the bus. Bruce came bounding up moments later.

"Hey, glad you got her, man," he said between breaths. "I'll take her now."

The young man looked at me, then at Bruce, and back at me. "Do you want to go with him?" He calmly asked me.

I couldn't answer. I was still gasping for air. So I just shook my head 'no'.

Bruce was not a little man. He probably stood over six-four and easily weighed two-forty. With his shoulder-length hair he looked even more imposing. The young man facing him was slim, but taller than my five-four. I realized that if Bruce pressed the issue, I would once again be his.

The man spoke softly, "The girl does not want to go with you. So why don't you take a walk?"

"No need to be high and mighty," Bruce said sarcastically. "There's more than enough to go around." As he spoke he grabbed for me.

Looking back on it now, I cannot say I saw the blow. The smaller man moved like lightning. The next thing I saw was Bruce on his knees holding his chest, with blood coming from his mouth. The blood was awful, but I was awed by the smaller man's ability. He moved with such precision and skill. Then everything went black. I must have passed out again.

Day 3 - Morning

When I woke the next morning, I was in a bed in a hotel room. I did not remember getting a hotel room. I was confused. Then the events of the night before came flooding back. I tried to sit up. I felt like my head was coming off, and my vision was not exactly clear. All I could do was lie back down and remember how foolish I had been for drinking so much. I decided at that point that I would never be a drinker. Then he came in from the bathroom.

"Awake I see, and still under the weather."

I just groaned, "Go away."

"Well, I really don't have anywhere to go." He grinned, a big stupid grin like a cat that had eaten a canary.

Now I really felt stupid; I was in his room. What was I doing in a strange man's room anyway? Then I remembered that he had saved me from Bruce.

"How did I get here?"

"I carried you. You didn't have a purse or any ID. Apart from a little cut on your head, you didn't seem to be hurt, other than being passed out and reeking of booze that is. I didn't want to leave you lying on the street."

While he was talking I became aware of the fact that I had on nothing except the bed covers. Now I was worried. What had gone on after he had rescued me? I couldn't remember anything.

"I can see how that was probably for the best," I replied, but then, after reflection, "You must have enjoyed removing my clothes."

He flushed red with embarrassment. "Not really.

Actually, I put you to bed in your dress, but after you puked all over yourself, and the bed, I had to clean you up."

I knew it was true. Somewhere in my alcohol-laced dreams I could remember being sick. Now it was my turn to be embarrassed.

"Your dress is in the bathroom," he continued. "I washed it and hung it up to dry. It was a little more difficult getting my hands on another set of sheets and making up a fresh bed for you."

"Do you have any aspirin? I think my head is about to fall off."

"I have something better. It's called a hangover kit." He handed me a small, medical pill envelope with six pills.

I looked at the pills, then at him. "What are these?"

"The big ones are APCs, and the little white ones are some type of vitamin B something-or-other. The rest, I'm not so sure. But they're not poison, and every time I've used them they've helped."

I just looked dumbly at the pills while he went to the bathroom and got me a glass of water. I made a decision as I watched him come back: even if they were poison, they'd put me out of my misery. It took me several minutes to take the pills, one at a time. I had a horrible taste in my mouth to begin with, and some of the pills were bitter.

"Who are you?" I asked.

"Jack. Jackson P. Jakes." He was grinning again.

"And who is Jack Jakes, when he is not rescuing maidens in distress?"

"Staff Sergeant Jakes, United States Marine Corps. At

your service, Ma'am."

I made a face. His grin went away. He knew something he'd said had displeased me.

"Is the lady going to introduce herself?" he asked.

I was really only functioning on half a circuit, but I managed to respond, "Pamela Sue Marks, student and war protester."

"Well, I guess that explains it."

"Explains what?"

"That look I got when I told you I was a marine."

"What look?" I replied, knowing he wasn't fooled by my innocent tone.

"The look like you just found a spider in your soup."

Well, he had my number.

"I guess I am a little surprised to find that I'm in the room of a soldier."

"Marine!" He interjected.

"Sorry, I guess I don't know the difference."

"There is a big difference."

"Like what?"

"Marines are actually part of the navy, and we fight from the sea, or any other place the army won't. The army mainly fights on land and is a large force composed of many divisions, while the corps is a small unit held together with esprit de corps. We're an elite fighting force."

Oh, my head hurt! He said too much and it didn't make any sense to me at the time. "What time is it," I asked for lack of any real reply to what he had said.

"Almost eight-thirty."

"May I use your bathroom?"

He stepped back from the bed, flung out his hand and bowed. "Your throne awaits, Madam."

I giggled in spite of the situation. I tried to sit up, but my head was still trying to fall off. I held out my hand, and he took it and steadied me. After a second try I was able to stand. With one hand I clutched the sheet around me, and with the other I gripped his hand tightly and slowly walked, step-by-step, to the bathroom. Once inside, he left me and closed the door. After taking care of my immediate needs, I stood and looked in the mirror. What a ghastly sight! No make up, hair standing on end, eyes bloodshot, and a bruise on the side of my face; a reminder of how close I had come to being seriously hurt. I looked at myself and wondered what Jack must think of me. I'm a realist, and there is no way anyone could ever consider me beautiful. For one thing, I'm too skinny, but I could still be considered pretty or cute, but probably not at the moment!

Turning away from the mirror I saw that my dress was hanging over the shower stall along with my slip and bra, just as he had said. They were almost dry. My sweater was there too. I moved my clothes, so they'd be out of the way, and got into the shower. It took a long time for the hot water to start working its magic on my abused body. Finally, after soaping myself for the third time, I started to feel clean. After drying off, I put on a robe I found hanging on the back of the door.

Jack was sitting over by the window reading the paper and drinking coffee when I came out. He had poured a second cup, and he pushed it over to me automatically. I wasn't much of a coffee drinker, but with sufficient cream and sugar it tasted pretty good. I was starting to feel almost human again.

"Don't the marines go to work at first light?" I asked.

"Sure, normally, but I'm on leave."

"Leave?"

"Vacation, to you. Leave is short for Authorized Leave of Absence."

"You don't go home for vacation?"

"Well, home, before the corps, was an orphanage."

"Oh, I'm sorry." I replied without thinking.

"Don't be sorry. There's no need. My father was killed in the Korean War when I was a baby, and my mother died in an automobile accident when I was seven. Jesuit priests ran the home I ended up in. I was raised by some of the finest men on the face of this planet."

"Why weren't you adopted?"

"Don't really know; I guess the right people never found me. After a while I was too big, and no one wants to adopt a half-grown, teenaged boy." He took a sip of his hot coffee before continuing, "What's with all of the questions?"

"I don't know. Just curious."

"So, Pam, when you are not protesting the war, what do you study in school?"

"I haven't really decided yet whether to major in History or English."

"Either one would be a good choice."

"Am I keeping you from anything?"

"Not really. Anyway, it's always nice to talk with a pretty girl."

"Even one who doesn't know the difference between the

marines and the army?"

"Sure."

Silence hung in the air. It seemed we had run out of things to talk about. I looked at him closely for the first time. He was lean, and probably just under six-foot. His chest and shoulders were bulky; he was in good physical condition. He was well-tanned, which was unusual for this time of year. He had short, dark hair. His jaw line was prominent-looking, chiseled; a thick shadow of a beard indicated heavy growth. He appeared to be appraising me, looking through piercing brown eyes that seemed to be laughing at me.

"What were you planning to do today?" I asked.

"Thought I'd walk out to the Mall and visit some of the museums and maybe the Lincoln Memorial."

Suddenly, I knew that I had just been delaying the inevitable. I didn't want to go back and face the other kids after what had happened with Bruce last night. I wasn't sure what they'd think. What would they say?

"Would you mind if I walked along?"

"Not at all," he replied. He seemed glad to have my company.

"It will take me just a few minutes to get ready."

"Take your time. There's no rush on my part."

I went back into the bathroom. I was beginning to feel better; the pills he had given me must be doing some good. I looked in the mirror. I didn't have any of my things with me, but I did the best I could do with what I could find. I used a rubber band to put my hair in a ponytail and pinched my cheeks to give them some color. Only when I started putting my dress on did

I realize that it had been ripped. He had sewn it, and had done a pretty good job of it, too. I still felt weird not having any panties.

We walked down one flight of stairs to ground level and out into the sunshine. It was a beautiful day. I still needed my sweater, but it was nice outside.

"Where does your family live?" he asked.

"Carbondale, Illinois. It's a small town in the southern part of the state."

After a couple of blocks we reached the Mall. We turned and started walking toward the Capitol.

"Where to first?" I asked.

"The American Heritage Museum."

"The what?" I'd never heard of it.

"The American Heritage Museum," he repeated. "A collection about the history of our country."

"Remember," I replied, trying to sound all-knowing and suave, "I'm not particularly impressed with this country at the present time."

"So, what country are you impressed with at the present time?"

"I don't know, but we are certainly not doing such a good job."

"Well, until something better comes along, I'll stick with this one."

"You have to say that; you're in the service."

"I am a volunteer, and on my second enlistment. If I had wanted to quit being a marine, I had my chance to quit. I'm a marine because I want to be."

"I don't understand that, especially with all the ill will towards the military because of Vietnam."

"Well, it is a free country, and everyone is entitled to his own opinion," he stated. "Even when it's wrong."

Now I was insulted. This obviously uneducated fool had the nerve to insult the highly educated and respected people who'd expressed their more learned opinions on the war. But I held my tongue. If I argued with him now I'd have to go back to my bus, and I wasn't ready for that yet.

We reached the museum, and he paid for my admission without asking. I didn't have my purse, so I couldn't even offer to pay for myself. For the next few hours we wandered through the exhibits. I saw for the first time the flag that had inspired Francis Scott Key; I learned that there had been battles on the Great Lakes; and I was introduced to colonial living. I had taken history in high school, but there was a lot I had forgotten. There was just so much to see, it was overwhelming. What I found the most interesting was the display of dresses of the First Ladies of the United States. It was interesting to see how the styles had changed during the last one hundred and seventy years.

We stopped for lunch in the cafeteria. By the time we'd finished eating, I was curious about Jack again.

"Is this what you intend to do on your vacation? Go to museums? I thought all of you in the marines were hard, two-fisted drinkers and the life of the party."

"There are some like that, but most are just regular folks. Some go to the library, some play chess, and some go to museums." He was smiling that big grin of his that irritated me. He looked like he knew something I didn't. "Actually, it is just such a pleasure to be in a country where most everyone speaks English. It's a constant strain dealing with people who speak a foreign language."

"But, you're an invader in their country."

"No, we've been invited there by the legitimate government of South Vietnam. We are protectors, or guests, by invitation. But it's still tiresome struggling with a language barrier."

We would never agree about the war. He was brainwashed by his training; at least that was my opinion at the time, so I changed the subject. "What did you find the most interesting at the museum?"

"I've always been interested in the period before the Civil War," he replied. "I liked that exhibit."

"But that was a time of real hardship. Women were treated like dirt. There was slavery, and the United States attacked Mexico." I criticized.

"Yes, but look at the advances in technology that were made. Free people pushed back the frontiers. The US gained most of its land during that period." Jack countered.

"That period created some of the problems that led up to the Civil War." I responded.

"Sure, but here again the Civil War actually resulted in the country becoming more technologically advanced. Railroads, telegraph, and breach loading guns were perfected."

"I guess only a marine could see a technological advancement in better ways to kill." He was starting to be really irritating again. "I cannot see the time before the Civil War as a great period; you only have to look at slavery and our wonderful treatment of the Indians." I shot back, my voice dripping with sarcasm. "So much oppression."

"Listen, slavery was a way of life long before the United States was created. Anyway, we were pikers compared to some other countries' treatment of slaves. Of course, if you are a slave, nothing is easy. The slavery issues needed to be resolved. It's just unfortunate that it took a war on the scale of the Civil War to resolve it. As far as the Indians are concerned, sure, they got a raw deal, but so has everyone in history who has lost a war. The winners write history. To the victor go the spoils."

"That is so hard and callous!" I was incredulous.

"Most truth is hard. But the last time I checked, there was no guarantee that things in life would be fair."

"Well, there should be," I insisted.

"Hey, life sucks and then you die. That's just the way it is."

"Is that the attitude you get from being an orphan?"

He looked at me long and hard before replying, "This Carbondale must be delightful; maybe I'll visit someday. Every day must be like a day at Disneyland, so nice and comfy. Shall we see the rest of the museum?"

I guess I'd finally gotten under his skin somewhat. He seemed to be calling for a truce for now. We wandered through the rest of the displays without much conversation, then we went back out onto the street.

As we walked up the Mall past the White House, I could see the pickets walking in the distance. Actually, it was quite a walk in the afternoon sun, and I was soon sweating and wanted to slip off my sweater. Jack helped me take it off, and then he carried it just as if I expected him to be a proper gentleman.

When we got to the Lincoln Memorial I was surprised by the enormous size of it. I had seen many pictures, but I could not have imagined the effect of the memorial without having seen it in person. I couldn't decide if I was more awed by the massiveness of the structure or the impressive artistry of the carving. Walking up the steps toward Mr. Lincoln sitting in his grand chair was overwhelming. He looked so life-like that I almost felt he was going to get up and talk.

While I was looking at the statue, Jack was reading the inscriptions on the walls. I joined him. On one side was the Gettysburg Address, and on the other side, Lincoln's second inaugural address. Reading them there, in that sacred place, the words rolled over me like a great wave.

"Those are inspiring words," Jack said in a soft voice, "The man was hurting. Think of all the deaths weighing on his conscience."

"I had to memorize the Gettysburg Address in junior high school. I don't think I ever really understood what it meant before now. It was just words then."

"I know what you mean," he responded.

Walking back down the stairs, looking at the George Washington Memorial in the Reflection Pool, I was filled with a renewed sense of hope.

"Would you like an ice cream?" He asked.

"Sure. Chocolate, would be great!"

He smiled and bought us each a cone from a vender on the street. We sat together on the steps, eating the cool refreshing treat.

"Thanks for saving me."

"You're welcome."

"Sorry it took me so long to thank you, but you keep making me so mad." I really did want to make amends.

"I don't mean to make you mad, but you sure have a funny way of looking at things," he observed.

We were starting up again, so I replied with the most neutral statement I could think of, "I guess we will have to agree that we disagree."

"Okay, if that's the way you want it. So, where do I take you now?"

I hesitated. I did not want to go back near Bruce, but I needed my clothes. I now understood many of the things my father worried about. I could still hear him: 'A girl alone is just asking for trouble!' I realized Daddy was right.

Jack must have realized my predicament. "Would you like me to walk back with you?"

I looked down, nodding my head. "Yes." I could not look him in the face.

Day 3 - Afternoon

When we got back to the area where the protest buses were parked, we found only a few people around. Betty was there sitting with some of the guys. They were painting new signs. I went into the bus and started looking for my suitcase. Betty followed me.

"Where have you been?" She asked.

I was leery of saying too much. Nothing had gone as planned so far, and my friends already seemed distant for some reason.

"I got sick," was my reply.

"Who's the jerk?" Betty asked, motioning towards Jack.

I looked out the window at Jack. He was watching the sign-painters. Jack certainly stuck out in this crowd. His hair was cut close, and his clothes were clean and pressed. Even though he was wearing a loose shirt, his bulging muscles, particularly his chest, made him stand out from the other guys. He might have been taken for a college student five or six years ago, but now he looked square. He was definitely not hip-looking. Suddenly it dawned on me that his clothes had probably been bought years ago and had been in storage for a long time. As a marine, he probably wore civilian clothes infrequently. It was apparent that he was unaware of current fashions.

"He's my friend. He helped me."

Betty shook her head in disgust. She obviously did not approve of Jack. I realized that my suitcase was missing, and there was no sign of my sleeping bag either.

"Where's my suitcase?"

"If you must know, Bruce has it. He told us what you did last night." Her tone of voice said it all. She was highly critical of me for some reason.

"What I did?"

"Yes. He wants his wallet and money back. He said that he would hold on to your things until you came back. I saw what you did to him. What did you hit him with?"

"I ... Me?... His wallet?... That son of a bitch..."

"He says you're an immature brat from a capitalist upbringing who has no idea about the higher purpose we're trying to serve here. He doesn't really care about his money, he called it trash, but you obviously have some problems that he needs to talk with you about. He figures that by holding on to your bag he will get the chance."

Now I was really frightened. Over the past few months, like so many of the other students, I had come to respect and admire Bruce. He was quite charming. He was actually a graduate student, political science, from what I recalled. Graduate students teach a lot of freshmen undergraduate classes, so he was actually a teacher, too. Then I remembered that he was expected to become a professor at the school. He had influence with the students, and he knew how to use it.

"Bruce tried to rape me! He lied to you."

"Get real, girl. Any girl here would be glad to jump in the sack with him at a moment's notice. This is the Age of Aquarius–free love." There was that term again: 'free love'. I was getting sick of hearing it. Our conversation was getting more bizarre by the moment. She continued before I could respond, "He told me how you tried to give yourself to him. He said you were drunk, and that in a fit of rejection you hit him with a pipe or something. When he came to, you were gone, along with his wallet."

I felt sick to my stomach. I could see in her eyes that she really believed his ridiculous story. Bruce was still her hero. Betty had been my friend since I had arrived at college. Now months of friendship began to dissolve.

"You know me. I don't lie or steal," I pleaded.

Her eyes told me she did not believe me. "Go ahead and believe what you want, even if it is a lie!"

I stormed off the bus. I did not want to talk with anyone.

I was so mad! I just picked a direction and started walking. Jack followed silently. I'd gone quite a way before I realized he was following me. I'd walked almost halfway back to the Lincoln Memorial.

Finally he asked, "Where are you going?"

I couldn't answer him because I didn't have a clue where I was going. Bruce had told such lies that I was no longer welcome, even by my best friend. That Betty could believe his awful story just made me sick. My father was so angry with me that I couldn't go home – I had my pride. Pride was about all that I had. I had no clothes, no money, no place to stay, and no way to get back to school or home. It all overwhelmed me! I just sat down and cried. I don't remember sitting down on the park bench, or of being aware of Jack for the next few minutes. He must have given me a handkerchief, because when I looked up again I had one.

I had to think. I knew that Bruce wouldn't go to the cops, not after the incident on campus last fall. The students had staged a sit-in inside the student union building. It started with a planned protest against Dow Chemical. Dow had sent recruiters to the campus to hire engineers and technicians. These job fairs had been going on for years, and Dow was just one of the many companies who sent representatives to the campus. It had come to the attention of the council of 'Students Against the War' that Dow was manufacturing bombs and explosives for the war. Dow was a major supplier, which made them a prime target for a focused protest. The students moved into the job fair and staged a sit-in. Over three thousand protesters crowded into a building that was designed for maybe four or five hundred. Once the building was full, with protesters sitting everywhere, even in the halls and storage rooms, the students who couldn't get in sat on the doorsteps and the walkways, blocking access.

The campus police could not handle the situation. The state police were called. They arrived in full riot-gear. From everything I'd heard, they had come in swinging. I hadn't been there because I'd had a class to go to. The cops used clubs and cleared the building within fifteen minutes. Hundreds had been arrested; many more went to local hospitals with head wounds that needed to be stitched up. After that, I'd listened to weeks of ranting speeches. From that day on the cops were referred to as storm-troopers or pigs. In fact, on further consideration of my current situation, I knew that none of them would ever tell the police anything about me. Cops were the enemy.

Jack was still waiting. The man had patience, I'll give him that. It must have been his training. "What happened back there?" he asked.

I was finally settling down a little inside, so I told him what Betty had said.

"Bastards!" He sat down beside me. "You need to go the police. I'll go with you."

"No cops!" I was determined.

"Why not?"

"The police are just looking for an excuse to beat up some protesters and throw them in jail."

"You've got to be kidding!"

"Remember, you've been out of the country for a while. Things have changed."

We were very quiet for a while. As we sat there watching

the sun sink slowly in the western sky, I explained my hesitation to go to the cops. I found that Jack was a good listener. I told him about the student protests and my views on the police. I told him about the Dow sit-in and how it had turned violent. I even talked some about Daddy. The sun had set, and it was twilight. For a while, neither of us spoke, and I was lost in my thoughts and despair.

All my plans and expectations had unraveled, and on top of everything else, thanks to Bruce, I still didn't have any underpants. I knew I was just delaying the inevitable – I'd have to go crawling back to Daddy. I didn't even have a dime to drop into a pay phone to make the call.

"Listen, as much as I hate the prospect, I have to go back home. Can I borrow enough money to make a call? They will wire me some money."

"Sure, if that's what you want to do. On the other hand, I have to attend this formal thing on Saturday night. You're pleasant enough to look at, you can carry on an intelligent conversation, and I need a date. I don't know anyone else in town. If you'll stick around, I'll stake you to a bus ticket and a couple of meals."

"Such flattery. You shouldn't lay it on so thick." I said sarcastically, but with a smile. "Just what kind of a girl do you think I am? I know this is the age of free love and all, but after the other night I'm beginning to realize that those two words don't go together."

"You're right. There is nothing free about love. Listen, I don't think you're that kind of girl, or I wouldn't have asked. If I wanted that kind of girl, this isn't the right part of town to look in. This is strictly a no-sex deal; there are still two beds in that hotel room. I'm kind of lonely and would love some company, and you need a place to stay for a few days while you figure things out. Conversation will be sufficient."

The wind started blowing and I began shivering. Jack still had my sweater. He gently placed it around my shoulders, and I leaned in against him to shield myself from some of the wind. This gave me a few moments to consider his offer. Yes, it would be much better to get home on my own somehow; better than having Daddy bail me out of the fix I was in. A little time to think about everything would be welcome, too.

"Okay. You have yourself a deal." Then I thought of something, "How can you afford it? I don't suppose they pay marines very much."

"Don't worry. I have more than a year's worth of back pay."

"You mean they haven't paid you for over a year?"

"Oh, it's not as bad as it sounds. Remember, in the service I don't have to pay for food or a place to sleep. I draw a little off the books when necessary, but more than five dollars a month in script was a waste where I was. There was nothing to spend it on, and it was more likely to be stolen than spent. Since I didn't have any need for the money, leaving it on the books seemed to be the smartest thing to do."

"You could have been earning interest on your money."

"Well, the little I had, and the distance involved in getting it to a bank, probably wouldn't have been worth the effort."

Realizing how I awful I must look, I ventured, "All right, we have deal. That's settled, but I have a favor to ask. Can I get a little advance to get another dress and a couple of other things?"

"Sure, but let's go get some dinner first," he said.

"I am hungry, but this dress is really not presentable."

"Okay, let's go. You have any place special in mind?"

Day 3 - Evening

Two hours later, we arrived at the Flagship Restaurant. It was an elegant restaurant down by the river. We had taken a cab from the hotel, even though it was only a short distance away. Jack had made reservations, and it was nice to be immediately escorted to our table when we arrived. We were whisked right past groups of waiting people.

Jack was wearing a nice sport coat, and I had on a new dress. I finally felt presentable again. My dress was nothing fancy, but it was practical and would be appropriate for many situations. We had gone to a department store on the way back to the hotel. I probably could have gotten by with my old dress, but I desperately wanted something else to wear. Happily, while shopping for the dress, I also managed to get new underpants, a slip, and some panty hose. My mother disapproved of panty hose, but they're the most practical way for women to wear nylons. Oh well, what she didn't know wouldn't hurt her.

Across the table from me sat the young marine whose attitudes so infuriated me. Still, there was no denying that I was drawn to his gentle strength of character. Why had I stayed with him? It wasn't just to postpone the prospect of facing my father; I wanted to know more about Jack. I needed to understand what could make a man willing to fight and to kill. Maybe I could teach him that there was a better way.

"Wine?" the waiter had suddenly appeared. After all the liquor that I had consumed last night, just the thought of any more made my stomach lurch.

"No thanks," Jack replied. "The young lady is not old enough, and I don't care to drink without her."

"We have a large selection of non-alcoholic beverages."

"That will be fine," Jack said smoothly. "Would you like a cup of coffee, Pam?"

"Yes, thank you," I responded.

The waiter handed us menus. I opened it and looked. The prices were outrageous! The average main entrée was priced from five to ten dollars. This was a very expensive place.

"Jack, you don't have to buy me a meal that costs this much, especially after buying me over thirty dollars worth of clothes."

"Oh, don't worry about it. A friend told me that this was a good place to eat. I was planning to come here one night this week, and it's much nicer with your company."

"It's just that you've done so much for me already. Now that I see the prices, well…"

"If it makes you feel better, tomorrow we will eat at one of those McDonald's hamburger places that seem to be popping up on every other corner. I saw one down the street from the hotel. But, tonight, I'm having a big steak."

We were interrupted by the waiter returning with our coffee. Water was already on the table along with a basket of warm rolls. The waiter spent a few minutes taking our order and going through the standard questions about how we'd like our food to be cooked. I was surprised when Jack made no attempt to order for me. Typically, in finer restaurants, waiters always took the orders from the men, and the women were ignored. Maybe the new women's liberation movement was having some effect. I know Daddy would have ordered for us and that would have been that.

"Jack, how do you feel about women's rights?"

"Are you talking about the crazy broads burning their bras, or just women who want to take over men's jobs?"

"Well, this is obviously not going to be easy," I replied. "So, you think it's crazy for a woman to have the same rights as a man?"

"I was sort of under the impression that women already had the same rights as men." He spoke in a matter of fact tone which I didn't really like. "What I see as the objective of this women's liberation movement is that women want to be like men."

"No, not like men; equal to men. Why shouldn't a woman make the same salary as a man if she does the same work?"

"Well, there's no reason she shouldn't. But women are not men, and men cannot become women. There are some basic biological differences that just can't be ignored."

"Aren't women denied equality in the marines? Are there any women generals in the marines?"

"No, there aren't. But there are also no women who have served in combat. In the military, combat is our primary function. Anyone who wants to rise to the very top, as an officer or an enlisted man, needs to have earned his place by serving in combat."

"If women are excluded from combat, how can they earn

that? It's discrimination." I asserted.

"Well, sometimes it's simply a matter of physical strength, although I admit I've met some fairly strong women. But as far as combat goes, a unit needs to be cohesive. Mixed units don't tend to be unified."

"How can you know that if it hasn't been tried?" I argued.

Jack continued, "I read that the Israelis mixed men and women together in infantry combat units. The results were disastrous."

"In what way? Are you saying women can't kill?"

"No, I'm sure they can, but combat is about more than just killing; it's about the most basic of all human instincts: survival. There were a number of problems with the mixed units. Many of the male Israeli soldiers were killed trying to protect the women, rather than fighting alongside them. Sex among the ranks is another issue. It complicates things and can destroy the unity necessary for combat. Men and women don't belong together in combat."

"But, all we want is equality."

"Equality sounds like a nice philosophy, but it's not practical. No two people, men or women, are equal. The only equality we need is equal opportunity."

"Well, we can't prove ourselves if the marines won't give us the opportunity." I retorted in frustration.

"I guess that's true, but the marines is like a big club. Membership is limited to only the few who can qualify. Modern warfare takes teamwork, it's getting to be a science, and women are too much of a distraction. I don't believe that mixing women and men together would work without making some drastic changes."

"So, what's wrong with changing?" I asked.

"Nothing's wrong with changing if there is a reason to change. Remember, the military set-up we have has been very successful throughout the history of the United States. You shouldn't mess with a winning team."

"So, you completely object to women serving in combat," I stated.

"Actually, I object to anyone serving in combat unless it's necessary. If women do go into combat, I think they'd have to have separate combat units. Too many problems arise in a mixed combat unit; it's just not worth the risk."

We were interrupted by the arrival of a large pastry bun. I bit into the pastry, a cinnamon bun, and it was the most delicious thing I had ever tasted. "Wow!" It was a house specialty served before meals.

Jack was equally impressed, commenting between bites, "This is a piece of heaven." Finally, we both agreed on something!

We ate in silence for the few minutes that our delicious cinnamon bun lasted. The waiter came back and refilled our coffees. As I went through the ritual of adding cream and sugar, I noticed that Jack drank his black. I offered him the cream and sugar. "No thanks. I used to drink it with cream, but since cream is rarely available to me, I've had to learn to drink it black or do without coffee."

I picked up where we left off, "Jack, women's rights is something I'm very passionate about. In the early days of this country, a woman was the property of her husband or father. She married whomever her father decided she should, or at the very least, needed his permission to marry. Women weren't allowed to talk in public, or express opinions, and married women couldn't work outside the home. You can understand why equality is so important to us."

"I can see your point. Looking back at the history of the suffrage movement, there were a lot of obstacles that had to be overcome before women were allowed to vote and own property. During World War II women proved they could do a lot of tough jobs. I do think women should receive the same pay if they're doing the same job that a man does. But I am still not sure that putting women in combat should be considered progress. Somehow, it seems that combat is the wrong forum to use for comparison in distinguishing the sexes. After having been in combat, I would certainly oppose the drafting of any daughter of mine for combat duty."

"Why, because you don't think she could do it?"

"No, but I just don't think women need to get down into the grit of the world. In combat, women wouldn't be respected, and they would be vulnerable to the abuses of the enemy."

"Combat duty aside, you have to agree that there is still oppression of women here, and in other parts of the world."

"You're right. There is still oppression of women, especially in other countries. But I think, and hope, it's getting better. Also, I hope that in this quest for equality, women don't lose what makes them so special. I'll tell you something that's true. If you want to start a fight in the corps–just say something bad about someone's mother! I'll give your ideas some thought, but you have to consider my perspective as a marine, too," Jack bargained.

"Fair enough, for now." I wasn't sold on his philosophy, but I was ready to let it go for the moment and enjoy myself.

Dinner arrived, ending this discussion. He had one of the biggest steaks I had ever seen. I had fish, Mahi-Mahi, and it melted in my mouth. I'm usually not real big on vegetables, but those that came with my fish were so tender and sweet. I wish I knew what kind of sauce covered them. Campus food, in general, is terrible. Eating on campus is at best a hit-and-miss situation. I think the main reason so many of the students are so thin is that the college's food is so bad. After we worked our way through our meal, the waiter was back.

"Dessert anyone?" The waiter asked.

I was so full I cringed at the thought. "No." We both replied in unison, which started us laughing at the coincidence.

"The bill, please," Jack replied. "I think we need to walk off some of this luscious meal."

"Very well." The waiter was all business now. He came back with the bill, and Jack laid his money on the little tray.

Once outside, Jack asked, "Would you like to walk along the river for a bit?"

The weather was warmer than it had been the other day, even though it was after dark. I was quite comfortable with my sweater on, and I was glad that I'd managed to hang on to it in all the commotion of the night before.

"A walk would be nice," I answered.

Jack smiled. "I understand the walk along the river is lined with cherry trees and is lit up nicely."

"Okay, let's go," I replied. "I'm sorry that I keep bringing up subjects that seem to start such heated discussions."

"I don't mind," Jack answered. "Actually, it's refreshing to have some stimulating conversation for a change. When everyone agrees with you all the time, it gets boring after a while. That's a problem in the corps. If something is confrontational, then there is always another marine ready to shout down your opinion. So there's no actual exchange of thoughts or opinions."

Jack was right; it was a nice area to walk in. As we walked, I reached out and took his hand. It felt so natural. It felt good–I was safe. I hadn't felt like this since I was a little girl with Daddy. The walkway along the river was lit up beautifully. We followed the path and looked at the lights and the river traffic. The sounds of the city filled the background. Finally, we came to a look-out area, and from there we had a beautiful view of one of the bridges.

"Remember, I have to go to a dinner party on Saturday night. It's a very formal affair."

"How formal?" I asked.

"Well, very formal. We will have to get you another dress. This will be a marine-thing, lots of military brass. I'll be wearing dress blues."

"Brass?" I was unsure what he meant.

"High ranking officers. Some important civilians will be there too."

"Okay, a deal's a deal. But right now I'm getting a little chilly. Could we go back now?"

We walked out to the street where a line of cabs waited. We took one, and we were back at the hotel within minutes.

Day 4 - Morning

When I woke the next morning, Jack was asleep on the other bed. I just lay there watching this strange man. His sheet had dropped down some, and I could see his exposed back. All at once I realized what I was looking at; he had scars on his back, some old, and some new. Some were obviously bullet wounds, but there were others that were long and ragged. Had they been caused by a knife, or by something else too horrible to imagine? There were marks that indicated some pretty serious cuts that the man, or maybe Jack as a boy, had suffered. Looking closely at his visible arm, I could see there were more scars that looked like bullet wounds. I knew that's what they were because my grandpa had bullet scars too. He had been a soldier in World War II.

Jack rolled over, opened his eyes, and looked directly at me. "Good morning," he said with a big grin.

This was the first time that I had ever awakened in the same room with a man. Well, it was the second time if I counted the day before when I was so sick. I decided that didn't count.

He sat up, covering his chest with a sheet. "You can use the facilities first. I'll call for some coffee."

Ten minutes later when I came from the bathroom, he was dressed in slacks and a tee shirt. I realized that even though we had been together a lot during the past few days, he had been careful not to let me see him without a shirt on. He must be self-conscious about his scars.

Jack was looking at a map, so I asked, "Well, what are we doing today?"

"Have you ever been to Mount Vernon?"

"No," I replied. "Isn't that George Washington's home?"

"That's right. I have a buddy who has a car, and he promised to loan it to me. We can have some breakfast, take a quick walk to Marine Barracks to get the car, and we'll be off to Mount Vernon."

"Okay," was my reply. It was his vacation; I was just along for the ride.

An hour-and-a-half later, we arrived at Marine Barracks at 8th and I streets. The compound took up several blocks of town. Jack showed his ID and another paper to the sentry at the gate. The marine on gate-duty was wearing a green dress-uniform that looked freshly ironed, and he was all business. Jack passed through the gate immediately after showing his ID, but everything came to a halt when the sentry demanded some ID from me. Jack explained that I had lost my purse and said he would vouch for me . That didn't make the least impression on the guard, and he called in the Sergeant of the Guard. Jack told him that we were going to see Gunny Callahan, and that made all the difference in the world. I was allowed to sign-in on the log with my name and address. Another column listed the fact that I was a guest of Staff Sergeant Jakes.

The place reminded me of a college campus. The lawns were cut, and the bushes were neatly trimmed. The landscaping rocks were painted white. All of the offices had little red signs with gold lettering identifying who occupied each office. We walked down a row of buildings, then up a long flight of steps to the second floor. These buildings had been around for a long time. The sign at the top of the stairs read 'Gunnery Sergeant

Callahan – Knock, uncover, then enter if you dare.' Jack used his fist to pound on the wall by the door. I could see that the paint was worn there from frequent pounding.

Jack spoke in a loud voice as he opened the door. "Is this where they keep the Gunnys in wheelchairs?"

The man behind the desk looked up at us with the meanest expression I had ever seen. He was a little man, but he had many rows of ribbons affixed to his shirt. When he recognized Jack, he smiled.

"Well, well, if it ain't the man. Son, you're a sight for sore eyes." Gunny stood and shook hands with Jack. "What the fuck have you been doing?"

"Mostly catching up on my sleep. I'm crashed in a place downtown. Just moving around and seein' the sights."

"Beats humping the bush."

"Sure does. Kind of a break to be away from the crotch."

"Yeah, done it a few times myself. Don't worry; in a couple of days you'll miss the green machine an' you'll be back panting at the gate."

"That's probably as true as my heart beats, but leave is nice for a while."

Gunny motioned toward the coffee pot. "Coffee?"

"Sure." Jack turned to me for the first time. "Want some too?"

I nodded my head, yes.

"And who might this pretty young filly be?"

Jack made the introductions, "Gunny Emmett Callahan, meet Pamela Marks."

In two strides, Gunny crossed the room to me and shook my hand lightly, then kissed the back of my hand. He was quite gallant, not at all the old sourpuss he had seemed at first.

"Glad to make your acquaintance," I replied softly.

I was standing next to a board nailed to the wall. It had hooks on it with rows of gleaming white, thick ceramic mugs hanging from the hooks. The cups were aligned as if in a straight military-like formation. Gunny snatched two cups down and held them both in one hand; placing them under the spout together, he filled first one, then shifted slightly to fill the other.

Gunny handed me a cup first, then handed the other one to Jack.

"Do you have any cream and sugar?" I inquired.

"Certainly, young lady." He quickly took back my cup and added the requested ingredients. As he held the cup out to me, I almost felt his mind probing at my thoughts. His eyes looked me up and down, taking in everything about me. He seemed to approve of me as a fit companion for Jack, but I could see he still had his doubts. "So, where does this polite and well-mannered young lady come from?"

"Illinois," I replied.

The old man grinned; he sort of looked like a smiling leprechaun. "Been there once. Chicago sucks almost as much as this town."

"Oh, I'm from southern Illinois, as far away from Chicago as you can get. Right now I'm attending the University of Wisconsin."

"A little far from school, ain't we, girly?"

"We are sightseeing together," Jack quickly interrupted.

He did not want the conversation to continue. "How about loaning us that car you've been bragging about."

"Sure." The older man walked over to his desk, opened the top drawer, picked up a key ring, and tossed it to Jack. "It ain't much, but it will get you to wherever you're going. You'll find it parked down below in the space marked 'Gunny'. No idea how much gas is in it, but you can bring it back full."

"Thanks," Jack nodded. "See you in a few days."

"Don't forget about Saturday night. You have everything you need?"

"I'm all set. The corporal took care of me. Oh, one other thing, add Pam's name to the list of guests. She'll be with me."

"Okay," Gunny chuckled. "Have fun, you two birds. Jack, don't let this filly suck all of the lifer blood from you."

Twenty minutes later we were in the car and driving down the road. The car wasn't much as far as I could see. It was about fifteen years old, either a '54 or '55 Ford sedan. As I watched Jack driving, I realized that I might have trouble driving this car; it was a stick shift. He didn't seem to mind; he shifted effortlessly as we cruised through city traffic.

There was a lot of road work going on. The future beltway Interstate 295 was under construction. Washington DC was designed by a French architect to be a splendid city. He borrowed the style from French design, so the city has traffic circles at its main intersections. The intersections were designed with horses and buggies in mind, but the designer had a grand scheme, and he made the roads very wide – wide enough to handle our modern automobile traffic.

The problem with traffic circles is that they only go

one way. If you don't get over fast enough once you enter the circle, you can't exit onto the street you want to be on. Jack was swearing under his breath as he was forced to circle around twice on Washington Circle. We finally managed to get onto 23rd St., and we drove down to Constitution Avenue. I could see the Lincoln Memorial as we turned onto the avenue. Jack had the map and had only looked at it briefly before we'd left. This street took us behind the White House and past the north side of the Capitol.

"Have you ever taken a tour of the Capitol?" Jack asked.

I was rubber necking, taking in the scenes, so I was slow to answer. "No," I finally said.

"Maybe we can go there tomorrow."

"That would be nice," I agreed.

We drove past the back side of the White House, so I couldn't see the protesters. Still, I was looking for them. I wondered if Jack had intentionally stayed off Pennsylvania Avenue for that reason. If we had turned onto Pennsylvania, we would have driven right in front of the White House where my friends were trying to help the country. I was beginning to feel guilty. I came here to make a difference and to put an end to this terrible war. Now I was driving around just enjoying myself.

"How come you didn't tell your friend, Gunny, about my being a protester?" I asked.

"He would not understand."

"Why not?"

"The Gunny is from the old-school marines. He cannot understand anyone disagreeing with the official policy of the

United States."

"Is he such a mind-numbed robot that he must obey at all costs?"

"No, but as a 17-year-old kid he was part of the invasion force that went ashore on Iwo Jima in February of '45. He was among the fifty or so, of his company who walked off the island after more than thirty-seven days of fighting. I think he got his silver star there. But he was also in Korea as a sergeant. He was one of the Chosin Frozen; he lost four of his toes on one foot to frostbite in Korea.

"Chosin Frozen? You guys certainly have your own vocabulary."

"Didn't you take any history in high school? Didn't they talk about the Korean War?"

"Of course I took history, and I do know about the Korean War. It was another pointless war fought just so the industrial powers in our country could make money."

"I don't know where you get your ideas! Do you recall that the Chinese Communist troops attacked the American troops in the winter of 1950? The marines were outnumbered ten-to-one as eight divisions of the Chinese Red Army attacked. They forced the U.S. into a retreat along a long line to Chongjin, which is now in North Korea."

"The United States never fought China," I insisted. I was beside myself with this new information.

"Oh yes, several times. But the point is that Gunny lived through the hell of Iwo and Chosin. He knows that the protest movement takes needed support away from the troops, and that can lead to an eventual defeat in battle and the loss of a lot of good marines. Gunny sees these protests as the killing of marines, sailors, and soldiers, just as though the protesters were doing the shooting."

"But the movement is trying to bring the troops home and save them from being killed."

"That's your side of the argument. We have to live with the actual results."

I could not take anymore of this type of talk; we needed to change the subject. It was obvious that we were not going to agree, so I said, "You used a lot of terms back there that I did not understand."

"Like what?" he asked.

"Gunny said something like, 'humping the bush.' Is that something sexual?"

He laughed, "Naw! Humping is what grunts do. Grunts are marine infantry. Humping is walking with all of your field gear on during a sweep mission."

"Oh." I was somewhat disappointed. "So what's the crotch, or green machine?"

"Same thing. Both mean the corps or the marines."

"What was that he said about sucking your lifer blood?"

Jack chuckled before replying, "Lifers are guys like me and Gunny: career marines. Some guys get married and decide to stay home with the wife. He doesn't want you to take me from the corps."

Now it was my turn to laugh. Gunny had misread our relationship.

We got to the Woodrow Wilson Bridge just in time to be stopped four cars back from the drawbridge. Jack got out of the car and walked to the rail, so I followed. There was quite a view. Jack pulled the map from his back pocket and studied it for a brief moment.

"Washington's place must be just around the bend of the river." All we could see were lush green lawns and plantation-style homes on the riverbank to the south.

I allowed my gaze to take in all the scenery. Then I stopped and looked at the cove on the Maryland side. There were two navy ships sunk in the cove. "Look," I pointed. "The navy has ships over there just spoiling the view."

Jack looked at the map again. "Oxen Cove. That must be where the navy does salvage training for divers."

"It's beautiful here. The navy should go somewhere else."

"That's always the problem. No one ever wants the military around except when there is dirty work to be done. If you want to be safe, then the military has to exist somewhere. We probably wouldn't even have seen the wrecks if we hadn't stopped in the middle of the bridge."

Before I could reply, the alarm sounded, and the bridge began lowering. By the time we'd raced back and started the car, the bridge was down, and we were moving again. Once we'd crossed the Potomac River, we were in Virginia. We turned south, following the signs to Mount Vernon. The drive down George Washington Parkway was a scenic one. There were lovely homes along the route, and for most of the drive I could see through the trees and out across the river on the left side of the car. The actual distance from the bridge to the mansion was only eight or nine miles. It only took about three quarters of an hour to get there from the city.

"I hadn't realized just how close Mount Vernon is to Washington D.C.," I commented.

Jack replied, "I guess the general wanted the nation's new capital to be close to home. One of the privileges of being the guy in charge."

We pulled into the parking area and got out of the car.

"I don't think of him as being a general, just a great president." I said.

"Well, he was a great general before he was a great president, so I think about him as being a general first."

For the next few hours we walked the grounds and toured the house. I learned a lot of new things about our first president. For instance, he never took any pay for serving as Commander of the Army during the Revolutionary War. When he died, he freed his slaves. George Washington, more than anyone else, was responsible for the Constitution. One thing he wanted to ensure was that his soldiers and officers who had served in the revolution got paid for their years of service.

Most surprising of all, I discovered that George Washington was not a man from the rich British upper-class as I had been taught for so many years. He never went to school in England as others of influence in the colonial days had. He worked and studied to better himself, and he was a surveyor. He made his money on land speculation and then happened to marry well. Martha was a wealthy widow. By the time he died, Washington was one of the richest men in the United States, but for the most part, he'd earned it.

If I had a place like that to live in, I'd never want to leave it. The last thing we did was visit the graves of George and Martha Washington. We paid our respects and left.

Clouds were starting to gather as we got back on the parkway. We had not gone more than a mile when it started to rain. Jack had been driving in the right-hand lane, moving with the slower traffic. Suddenly, a large, dirty, brown Mercury came up alongside us on the left and abruptly swerved into us. Jack slammed on the brakes–so did the other car. Jack accelerated and went up onto the shoulder and around the Mercury. It came at us again, fast, from behind. Blam, the car shook as the bigger car slammed into our rear bumper, forcing me back into my seat, then forward against the dash. Jack sped up, throwing me back against my seat again. Then the big car came back up alongside us on our left. Wham! Wham! Wham! It slammed into us in quick succession. I looked up and saw a curve coming up; they were trying to force us off the road!

Jack said, "Hang on, baby! I'm gonna stop real fast. They've got more engine than we have. Can't outrun them."

I braced myself against the dash, then flew forward as Jack slammed on the brakes. We fell back and away from the big car, and Jack turned the wheel hard to the left. There was an intersection-opening in the highway. As we spun violently and slid across the intersection, I thought we were out of control and would wreck; but at the critical moment, Jack accelerated and we straightened up. We drove back down the highway in the other direction. We turned right into a development of nice homes. I looked back. The big Merc had turned around and was driving across the grass median, following us.

Jack drove up the street at breakneck speed. This was a

residential area; the speed limit had to be in the twenties. We turned right at the second street, then left and up another road. Jack weaved back and forth, speeding up, and then braking at the turns. Thank God there were no kids around! They must have been in school. Wham! The Merc rammed us again from behind. Jack turned sharply, and we briefly got away from the bigger car because it couldn't turn as tightly as our smaller car.

Then Jack made a mistake; he turned down a dead end street. We could see the end of the street as soon as we came around the corner. I gasped, and Jack cussed. I looked at him. He had a gleam of wildness in his eyes that sent adrenalin shooting through my body. Instead of stopping, he accelerated straight to the end of the street! Up a driveway we went, and then in between the houses. We hit some trash cans and then turned to the left, crossing through the yard behind the house. The bigger car could not make the turn and slid into the bushes. I looked up as we hit some laundry on a clothesline. We went under it and only knocked off a pair of pants. We turned left again, going back around the other side of the house. We dropped off the curb, causing me to bite my tongue. Then we were going back down the street. I only got a brief glimpse of the big car, which was still in the bushes. Somehow Jack had kept his bearing, even with all of the turns. A few turns later we were back on the parkway.

At the next intersection we turned left and pulled to a stop beneath a railroad bridge.

"Watch for that asshole while I look at the map."

He was studying the map when I saw the Merc going up the parkway at high speed.

"Just went past!" I called out.

"Good, there's another way out of here going over to U.S.-1. We'll go that way."

"Okay!" I was breathless. "What was that all about?"

He looked at me as he put the car in gear. "I don't know. I was hoping you might have some ideas."

I shook my head. "I'm too scared to think. Jack, can we just go?"

"I'm scared too," he replied calmly, "We'll take the long way back."

Day 5 - Morning

It was a beautiful morning, the sun was out, and I was on my own. Jack left early before I woke up. He left a note telling me to have breakfast, and that he would return between nine and ten. He had also thoughtfully tucked two dollars in with the note to pay for breakfast. The hotel had a quaint café with outdoor seating.

I spent a dime on a copy of the morning paper and caught up on the news for the first time since leaving school. Senator Eugene McCarthy seemed to be winning the Democratic Primary in New Hampshire. Most of the kids liked McCarthy, but I still wasn't sold. McCarthy is running on an anti-war platform and challenging President Johnson. The reality of it is that if an incumbent president wants to be re-elected, he will be re-elected. As unbelievable as it sounds, Richard Nixon is the leading Republican. I can't believe there's any chance he'll be elected.

General Westmoreland requested more troops for duty in Vietnam. Clark Clifford was named our new secretary of defense. Wasn't he one of President Truman's advisors? Thousands of Polish students were rioting in Warsaw. I hoped those kids would remember what happened in Hungary in the '50s; the Soviets rolled in tanks to quell the riots. There was some problem brewing about the price of gold. No American can own gold anyway, so I don't understand the problem. Secretary of State Dean Rusk is to review the current Vietnam policy. About time! Well, at least the comics page had reliable things to read. I always read L'il Abner and Dick Tracy. Blondie and Mary Worth are good too, but I must say the new cartoon,

Peanuts, is the best.

After I finished breakfast I continued to sit and read while drinking coffee. The cafe was nice, but crowded. The hotel had been around for a long time. I could tell that it had received several face-lifts over the years. The chandeliers had originally been piped for gas. It was old, but clean.

I looked up and Jack was standing there, smiling, and holding a garment bag with the marine crest on it, and 'USMC' in bold letters below the crest.

"I'll run up and put this away, then we can go."

"Okay," I replied.

I opened the paper to the editorial page. There was a long article written about draft deferments. It seems that the National Security Council had abolished draft deferments for most college graduate students. Just the thought of that makes me fume. Why waste the best minds in our nation? It has to stop! Can't the president see what is happening? The nation is being torn apart at the seams.

Jack was back and ready to go. I was glad because I couldn't take any more of the news. I took his hand as we walked down the street toward the Capitol.

"Where have you been this morning?" I asked.

"I put the car in for repairs and went to the Marine Barracks to get my uniform."

"Why did you put the car in for repairs? Doesn't your friend have insurance?"

"He probably does, but he was not driving; I was, and I am responsible for the damage."

"Everything you say makes sense, but it always seems to

have an odd twist to it."

"There is no twist. There is just right and wrong. If you do something wrong, you make it right. I don't know any other way."

His attitude was not at all what I am used to with my college friends. It really gave me something to think about.

"Why do you need your uniform? I thought you were on vacation."

"I have to wear it to the dinner party tomorrow night. As a matter of fact, this afternoon we are going to get you a nice dress for the party."

We visited the Capitol and took the standard tour. It was interesting to hear about how the building had changed over the years. I learned that the construction of the great dome had continued during the Civil War. In the midst of all the destruction and loss of life, something so beautiful had been created.

Just stepping into the rotunda was a breathtaking experience. Eight glorious and priceless paintings hang on the walls surrounding visitors; Declaration of Independence and General Washington Resigning His Commission are the most impressive of them. But then you look up at the ceiling and the painting takes your breath away! The underside of the dome is a great work of art done in fresco. It's called the Apotheosis of Washington. It depicts George Washington sitting between Lady Liberty and Lady Victory. Figures representing the thirteen original states complete the inner circle. Dominating the outer circle is the sword-wielding Lady Freedom. Other groups symbolize the glories of agriculture, mechanical engineering, science, art, and commerce.

I was surprised to learn that the British, during the war of 1812, had nearly burned the Capitol building down. In August of 1814, British troops invaded the city and set fire to all of the public buildings. The British officer who led the attack sat in the 'speaker's chair' and proclaimed 'Shall this harbor of Yankee democracy be burned.' His troops then set fire to the building. The Capitol building was literally gutted and would have burned completely to the ground if it hadn't been for a freak rainstorm which put out the fire. Of course, the Capitol building was not nearly as large then as it is today. It's frightening to realize that it could be attacked again, and this time it could be done with a nuke.

The room that was originally the House chambers is now the National Statuary Hall. On display are impressive life-sized statues of great Americans from each of the fifty states. I remember learning in school about the great men who gave so much to found this nation, and seeing the protesters through the windows, I couldn't help but wonder if the final chapter of this nation was being written.

After the tour, we walked out where we could look up the Mall toward the George Washington and Lincoln Memorials. It was broad daylight, and I knew the protesters were still out front, but it didn't matter to me anymore. I was just a little chilly in the cool breeze, and Jack put his arm around me, so I slipped my arm around his waist. It felt good. He drew me close and kissed me. This was the first time I had ever been truly kissed. Oh, I'd been kissed before, but never by a man whom I loved. I could feel it all the way to my toes. As a matter of fact, I can still feel it, weeks later.

"Sorry," he said as we broke apart.

"Don't be," I replied. "I wanted it as much as you did. I just didn't know it." So he kissed me again. It felt as good as the first one.

Down the steps we went, hand in hand. We went into town and spent the rest of the afternoon shopping. He was looking for a nice dress for me to wear on his special night.

****

At this point I need to interject the details of an earlier incident. While I was sitting around enjoying breakfast, Jack had been busy. Despite my objections he had gone to the police. The narrative that follows is what he related to me:

Jack went to the police headquarters of the District of Columbia, and told the desk sergeant about what had happened on the road with the Mercury. He asked if he could talk to someone who could help. The sergeant asked where the incident had occurred, and when Jack told him, he said that it was out of their jurisdiction and to try the Park Police or the Virginia State Troopers.

Jack was about to leave when another man in civilian clothes stopped him and asked, "Haven't I seen you before?" Jack told him he didn't think so, but the man was persistent. "Wasn't your picture in the paper? Some article about the marines or something?" The man picked up the paper, leafed through it, and found the article. He obviously had a memory for fine details. He invited Jack to join him for a cup of coffee.

Detective Larry Thomas led Jack back to an area with vending machines. Jack told him about the events of the past few days, starting with the attack on me. When he finished, the detective just sat there. Jack said he had to prompt the detective, "So, what do you think?"

"Quite frankly, I don't know what to think, but my gut feeling is that you or your girlfriend are on the outer-fringes of something. And this is a something that someone wants kept quiet."

The detective gave Jack his card, and Jack gave him our hotel room-number. He told Jack that if he could find out anything, he would be in touch.

Day 5 - Evening

When we returned to the hotel after shopping, Jack spent the afternoon teaching me how to play cribbage. Later, we got dressed for dinner and took a cab from the hotel to a restaurant. The restaurant was very nice. Jack was wearing his one-and-only sport coat and slacks. I, on the other hand, had a new pink dress, one that Daddy would never have approved of. He would have thought the skirt was too short (above my knees), and he wouldn't have liked the cut of the dress in back. It would have shown my bra strap if I had been wearing one. However, I did finally feel properly dressed.

Once we were seated, someone immediately filled our water glasses. The waiter was very prompt.

"I'm in the mood for lobster; how about you?" Jack asked.

I agreed, and the waiter was off to place our order.

"So, tell me about Vietnam."

He took a drink of water and gave me a long look. "You know, this is probably not a good subject for us."

"I know, but all I know is what I've seen on TV and what

has been discussed at school. You're the first person I've known who has actually been there."

"You want to know about the country? About the people? Or just about the war?"

"Actually, I'd like to hear a little about each. I don't think the war is about what I've been told."

"It's not. And we have both been told the same things: whatever the politicians on either side want us to hear, or think we can understand." Jack paused and took a sip of his water. I sensed that he was trying to gather his thoughts to say the right thing. I gave him time and just sat enjoying the pleasant aromas coming from the kitchen.

"The reasons for war, for the most part, are complex. On the face of things, it often seems that a single action can start a war. In truth, the tensions that precede war often build for a long time before flaring into war at a single incident."

The South Vietnamese are great! A lot of their culture has a French flavor to it because they were a French colony for a long time. Most of the people make us feel welcome; they want us there. The country is beautiful. You may think it's green around here, or in Illinois, but Vietnam is the greenest place I've ever been. It gets lots of rain, so something grows in almost every square inch of dirt."

"Then why is the country so poor?" I hated to interrupt, but I couldn't help but ask. "It would seem that they should be able to feed their country easily."

"Actually, the villages have been living off the land for centuries without any intervention."

"What is the war about?"

"Let me explain it in simple terms. You live in a small town in Illinois. Let's suppose the people of Canada reason that since colonial settlers were British citizens at one time, the people of Illinois are actually citizens of Canada. Initially, they just order us to pay Canadian taxes. At first everyone would just laugh at their ridiculous demand. But then, Canadian invaders come. They infiltrate and marry some of the girls in town. Some are even elected to city council. They try and force the council to swear allegiance to Canada. When the council refuses, other Canadians show up and take the mayor out into the town square where he is publicly subjected to torture."

"What kind of torture?" I interrupted again.

"You sure about this? It's not pleasant dinner conversation."

"Yes, I want to know."

"At first, just beatings and humiliation in front of his family and friends. If the man is tough and unwilling, they might rape his wife or daughter, or kidnap or kill his son. First sons play an important role in Vietnamese culture. Kidnapped first sons are often held in the north to ensure the good behavior of a village mayor. If that doesn't work, they'll make an example of him by cutting off parts of his body or leave him for dead with a hot rod run through his belly. Intimidation on a grand scale! It works because the people, for the most part, are simple hard-working folks just trying to get by."

"I still don't understand what we are doing there."

"You've got to look at the bigger picture. This war is just another example of bigger, more powerful countries trying to get control of the world. Are we going to be communist or capitalist republics? Vietnam is just one battle in the larger struggle. Communist aggression has to be stopped on all fronts. Whether it's the Soviets or the Chinese, they have to be stopped. It's better to stop them over there than wait for them to get here."

"But, North Vietnam is no threat to the United States."

"Well, it was not that many years ago that another aggressor just wanted Austria, so it was no threat to us when he took it. After all, Germany was no threat to the U.S. But then he wanted the Sudetenland. Next he invaded Poland. Then France. Finally a world war had to be fought to stop the aggression. We are now in the nuclear age; a world war now would result in tremendous devastation. Everyone knows this, the U.S. and Soviets especially, so we fight these limited wars."

He made sense, but I was stubborn and did not want to admit that he might be right about the U.S. involvement in the war. So I kept quiet, and I didn't have to respond because dinner arrived.

After dinner we went walking again. It was a pleasant spring night. Even though I had my sweater, I didn't really need it. In fact, Jack slipped off his coat and loosened his tie. This was Georgetown. Its narrow streets were built for carriages and horses, not automobiles. In its own rustic way it was very quaint. We walked hand-in-hand through several of the shops. There was one devoted to the hippie-type stuff seen in San Francisco, another to calendars, and one to music. You could hear the music a block away; they were playing a Beetles song. John Lennon is my favorite. It was obvious that behind and above the shops were apartments. I'll bet the neighbors loved the music!

We went into a shop filled with Chinese knickknacks

where Jack bought me a small glass rose. I had never seen anything so delicate. The sales lady carefully wrapped it in paper and tied it with string.

We left the shops and the lighted area behind us as we went up a street that looked strictly residential. Actually, we had to walk out in the street to go around piles of garbage. I could see down about two blocks, and there appeared to be an illuminated street ahead. So we walked on, holding hands, just enjoying each other's company.

"Maybe we can get a cab at the next street," Jack suggested.

"Okay."

Then it happened. Fortunately, Jack was much more alert than I was. As we stepped back into the street to skirt around another pile of trash, Jack pushed me down into the garbage and jumped on top of me. What kind of a prank was this? It wasn't funny, and it certainly wasn't romantic! Then I heard the squealing of car tires.

Jack was up off me; he jerked my arm, and I was up on my feet. He started to run, pulling me with him. "Move out!" Were his only words.

We ran back past the houses, then turned down an alley. Jack had me by the arm, pulling me faster. I could hear the tires as the car backed up and turned to follow us down the alley. I looked back over my shoulder for a fleeting second, just in time to see the headlights line up on us. Jack surged forward, almost pulling me off balance. He steadied me, and then I was running faster than I ever had in my entire life. I didn't know I could run that fast. As fast as we were running, we could still hear the car coming ever closer. We were running for our lives; at least I sure was.

Suddenly Jack jerked me sideways into a small opening, sort of a sub-alley not really big enough for a car. The left side of the car hit the edge of the opening. I heard the crunch of the car scraping on the bricks, and we were pelted with flying rocks and chips of brick. Jack found a door. He tried the knob, but it was locked. Across the alley, we tried another door. It didn't open either. Jack threw his shoulder into the door and it gave way. We hurried through it and found ourselves in a bar of the seediest type. It smelled of a mixture of stale beer, urine, and rotting food. We didn't stay long. We went out the front door.

A cab was sitting there, and Jack and I both jumped in. The cabby flipped up his meter as he pulled away from the curb.

"Took you long enough, Bud. Where you heading?"

"Downtown," Jack snapped.

"Hey, you ain't the same guy I was waiting on! There's already five bucks on the meter."

Jack pushed a bill through to the driver. "Don't look back. The other guy said I could take the cab."

I looked back just in time to see a man run out into the street and throw his coat down in anger. I realized I was breathing in wheezing-like gasps. I leaned forward, trying to catch my breath. Finally, when I could speak, I asked, "Was that an accident?"

"Chasing us yesterday could have been accident if they thought we were someone else, but chasing us like that tonight is pure intent to hurt or scare."

I whispered, "All right; I'm scared. You?"

"Nope. I was. Now I'm pissed!"

Day 6 - Morning

The Smithsonian Museum opened at ten o'clock, and we were there when it opened. It was a long and pleasurable day of wandering from one display to another. It was doubly enjoyable just being with someone who was nice, and easy to talk with. We ate lunch at one of the cafeterias in the museum. He told me funny stories, and he listened to my stories.

We started at the Castle. I was totally unaware of the quirky history of the museum. James Smithsonian, who died in 1829, was the illegitimate son of a Duke of Northumberland. He willed his entire fortune to his nephew, stipulating that should his nephew die childless, his fortune would instead go to the United States to establish a national learning center. He had never even been to the United States. Five years later his nephew died without heirs. A decade later, in spite of anti-British sentiment in the states and a suit contesting the will in England, the bequest was fulfilled, and the Smithsonian Institution was founded. In 1904, James Smithsonian's body was moved to Washington from Italy, and he was entombed in the castle building. What started with an unexpected bequest has become one of the most esteemed groups of museums in the world.

We walked down to the new American Art Museum. Not all sections were open to the public yet. We saw brand new displays. Further down the street we visited the National Archives, and I got to see the actual Declaration of Independence and the Constitution. Our last stop was the Museum of Natural History. It houses the most complete displays! Halls of rocks, fossils, bones, insects, spiders, and human artifacts. We wandered through exhibits showing American Indians and various living conditions of people on other continents. There were displays on anthropology, biology, geology, and oceanography. I felt more aware of the world and our history after that day. It was almost overwhelming. But what was most surprising was that it was all free.

Finally, Jack managed to haul me out. "We have to get ready for our big date," he said. "You need to be in condition to do some dancing."

Day 6 - Evening

I was dressed and ready to go! It had taken me hours to get everything just right. Jack told me that there would be photographers there, and I wanted to look my best, so I was very careful with my hair and makeup. I was surprised to find that it took a marine even more time to get ready, or as Jack termed it, 'inspection ready'.

Jack spent a long time spit shining his shoes. They looked pretty good before he started, but when he finished they were the shiniest shoes I had ever seen. It had taken a lot of cotton balls and hard work. He even shined the bill of his hat. Then he took his dress blues out of the garment bag and went over them with meticulous care, cutting off every loose thread he could find. Jack called the threads 'Irish Pennants'. He explained that the blues were new, and the threads had to be removed. Then he carefully polished the brass buttons and his belt buckle. Finally, he affixed all of his insignias and ribbons to the front left chest area of his jacket. He had four rows of ribbons.

When I asked what the ribbons stood for, he just replied off-handedly, "For good conduct."

This was the first time I'd had to wait for a guy. I watched as he finished dressing. He had to twist himself to get into his coat and fasten the neck clasps. He meticulously fastened his buttons before putting on the traditional marine belt. He turned to me and smiled. "You look quite beautiful. Are you sure that you want to be seen with a scruffy old marine? This is your last chance to back out."

"I've come this far. In for a penny, in for a pound, as the saying goes."

He handed me a blue box. I was unsure and excited at the same time. At first I thought he was offering me a piece of jewelry to wear. But then I saw the embossed words on the box: 'UNITED STATES OF AMERICA'. I opened the box carefully and looked inside. It took me a long moment to realize what I was looking at. It was the Medal of Honor.

Jack took the medal out of the box in a cavalier manner and placed it around his neck. "Check the back and make sure it's straight for me. There will be a high brass level tonight. I wouldn't want to hear about being out of uniform."

I'd never thought about a man being beautiful, but Jack was absolutely stunning!

He took my arm, and we went out the door. When we arrived in the lobby there was a young marine waiting for us. He had a pock-marked face, and only one stripe on his uniform.

"We are running a little late, Staff Sergeant. The car is out front."

The late model sedan was very clean. It had 'USMC' stenciled on the door, with a number just below that. The younger marine opened the door and waited for both of us to get in. Gunny Callahan was in the front seat.

"Good evening, Miss Marks. I hope you're hungry. I hear they lay out a lot of food." The Gunny was in dress blues also. He had even more ribbons than Jack had, but he did not have the medal around his neck. The driver got in and away we went.

"Good evening, Gunny! It's nice to see you again. Yes, I am hungry. Now will someone please tell me where we are going?"

"All in good time," replied Jack.

The young marine driver seemed to know the city well. When we approached the White House, I looked for my school chums, but they had apparently already gone back to the buses.

Suddenly, we turned in and drove up at the gate of the White House. "This is our special date?" I asked in amazement.

Gunny chuckled. When he spoke his voice rumbled with an Irish brogue. "Jack has a bit of the leprechaun in him. Likes to spring little surprises, does he not?"

The guard at the gate looked in the car with a flashlight. Gunny handed him a letter that had the U.S. Marine Corps crest at the top. The guard looked at Jack and said, "Staff Sergeant Jakes, welcome to the White House." He thrust out his hand, and Jack shook it. "I'm a marine too; got out in forty-six. With all this crap around here all day long, you make me proud. Good job Marine!"

"Thanks," Jack replied. He was obviously uncomfortable with his notoriety.

With that, the guard pushed the button on the gate and stepped back, allowing us to pass through.

As we drove up the driveway I made the simple inquiry,

"Why should a man who has been out of the marines for over twenty years be so interested in a young marine today?"

Jack coughed and looked embarrassed. Gunny answered, "Missy, once a marine always a marine!"

The doors of the car were opened immediately when the car stopped at the head of the driveway.

Jack held my arm, steadying me as we went up the steps into the White House. We were greeted by the president's chief of protocol. We were escorted down a long hallway and placed in line to meet the president. As each couple moved up the line, a young man would call out the person's name and title. I remember his announcing, "The Honorable Richard Ichord, congressman from the great state of Missouri."

The line moved very quickly and suddenly we were there. "Staff Sergeant Jackson Jakes and Miss Pamela Marks."

President Johnson shook Jack's hand, and the First Lady shook mine. The president spoke to Jack in his Texas drawl, "Glad you could join us for dinner, Sergeant."

"Thanks for the invitation, Sir."

The first lady took my hand saying, "Welcome to the White House, my dear. My, my, don't you look stunning!"

"Thank you," I managed to stammer nervously.

Then we were led into the Blue Room. I later learned that this room is routinely used for state dinners. A giant painting of George Washington dominated the room. The dining table was elegantly set for about thirty. We were escorted to our chairs about a third of the way down the table. We all stood behind our chairs until President Johnson and the First Lady entered. Once they had taken their places at the head of the table, we all took our seats.

Over to one side was a four-piece ensemble playing music. The musicians were dressed in marine uniforms. All-in-all, it was quite lovely. We were seated across the table from an army general and the congressman from Missouri.

Salads arrived first. I listened, while eating, as the army general carried on a conversation with the congressman about the tests on a new rifle developed for all services. At first I really didn't pay that much attention to the discussion; I was too busy concentrating on which fork to use.

The congressman was most verbose, "There's no question about it; more fire power, lighter weight, and a standard load compatible with NATO. That's exactly what we need. I'm pushing for restarting production as soon as possible."

The general replied, "I fully support the new weapon. However, let's find out if there are problems. More testing is needed."

"I've got volumes of tests from Colt, Smith & Wesson, and Remington. The M-16 is the gun of the future. Just what the army needs."

Jack was eating silently, but listening, too.

"Staff Sergeant Jakes," the general called to Jack.

"Yes, Sir."

"I understand that you got a chance to fire the M-16. I saw your picture from one of the photo sessions down at Quantico."

"Yes, Sir," Jack replied nodding.

"So what did you think of the gun?"

"It's a piece of junk." Jack took another bite without hesitating.

"See?" The general smiled at the congressman. "An unbiased opinion from a professional."

The congressman got red in the face. "Young man, I have reports, and we have done studies. I cannot believe that you have an informed opinion."

Jack laid down his fork and stopped eating. His eyes narrowed; he spoke softly, "Guess you're right, Sir. I'm only a mud-marine. Barely finished high school. But believe it or not, I can shoot. I've even had a confirmed kill at 350 yards; shot an NVA general. That could never happen with an M-16. You're basically shooting a 22. With a 30 caliber you have some serious knock down power. But my real problem with the M-16 comes from finding a group of army grunts—dead; killed with their weapons disassembled. They had been trying to fix the crap guns you guys gave them, and if the general here helped you, he is just as guilty as you are. If you are going to send men to fight a war, at least you can give them the proper tools."

The general inquired, "What would you recommend, Staff Sergeant?"

"I've been using a Stoner. Good piece. Fires belt feed as well as semi and auto. Decent range. I guess no congressman owned a piece of the company. Excuse me, I have to make a head call." With that, Jack stood and left.

Everything was quiet for a moment or so, then the general smiled at me. "Don't worry, he's not in trouble. Senior people should not ask a question if they don't want the answer."

"Is it true?" I asked.

"What?"

"That you and the congressman actually sent those boys

over there with guns that don't work?"

"Well, I'd like to say no, that we had nothing to do with it. Actually, that is why I have the job now; the guy who had the job before me made some mistakes. For whatever reason, the soldiers were given less than perfect weapons. But the good news is that I believe the problems they encountered have been solved. As a result, we actually have a better gun than we would have gotten from years of testing."

"It really seems like the wrong way to do things."

"I have to agree in this case – We sure were short on being right."

Jack came back and sat down just as we were interrupted by the collecting of salad plates and the serving of the main course. I can't say exactly what the dish was, but it was some sort of chicken, with potatoes and green beans. Everything was very good, although Jack did make some grumbling comment about the size of the portions. There were no more caustic conversations during dinner. Afterwards, I went to the ladies' room while Jack went with the men to smoke. I have to say, the ladies' room was one of the most spectacular bathrooms I have ever been in. There were little couches and built-in vanities in the outer area. There was even an attendant to hand out the towels.

I ran into Gunny Callahan in the hall. "I didn't see you at the table."

He just grinned and chuckled. "I'm just here to help the commandant and keep Jack out of trouble. They're not going to let me eat with the important guests."

"You're important," I insisted. "Heck, you've got more

ribbons than most of the generals out there."

"Don't worry about me; I ate just fine. They feed real good down by the kitchen. Anyway, it's not the ribbons or the medals; it's the man."

"I don't understand the ribbons. Would you explain them to me?"

Gunny looked perplexed, as if no one had ever asked him such a question. Finally, I guess he decided that I was not being intentionally rude. He started at the bottom and pointed them out while explaining, "The bottom rows are campaign ribbons indicating wars or service." He pointed to a multicolored red one and said, "This one represents World War II victory."

He moved his hand across the next row up. "These are awards everyone gets if they stay long enough: good conduct, unit citations, and so forth. The top rows are the personal awards. These distinguish the warrior from the others. The top one I have is the Silver Star. When you look at Jack, you will see that he has a star on his. That means he has two Silver Stars. The purple ribbon here is the Purple Heart. You get that for not keeping your butt down and getting wounded. Jack also has another purple ribbon with white in it. That is the Navy Cross. Our friend Jack is a real live hero. He deserves that Medal of Honor he's wearing tonight. Don't ask him how he got his medals – It's considered bad manners. Anyway, he will probably just lie. Just as I will lie if you ask me about my Silver Star."

"Why?" I inquired.

"Because war is a gruesome business at best, and the real heroes don't come home." He placed his hand on my cheek and said, "You're too pretty to waste time talking to an old marine. Go dance and enjoy yourself. Take your happiness when you can get it." He turned me and gave me a little shove. I remember that his hands were rough and calloused against my bare shoulders.

I walked back thinking that I really liked that old guy. Jack was speaking with the general again. The way the potted plants were arranged, I was able to come up where I could hear them before they could see me. I admit I was moving slowly to eavesdrop a little.

"Don't be so hard on the congressman," the general told Jack. "Actually he's nowhere near the worst of them. In a lot of ways he is better than most. Of course, we are all politicians here in Washington, even the senior military. But don't say politician like it's a four-letter word. Good politics is what gets things done in this country. That's the way it's been since we were founded. I've always found that there are two types of politicians: There are those that work hard at making themselves look good; if they do some good in the process, it's a lucky accident. Then there are the politicians who understand the give and take, and work the system to get the job done. If they look good as a result, then that's the accident. It does not make any difference which party they belong to, or which service. Every group has both kinds. I always try to be the second kind."

"So how do you tell the difference?" Jack asked.

"Oh that's easy." The general paused to put out his cigarette. "The first guys are always saying, 'I did this.' While the good kind will say, 'We did this.'"

I couldn't dally any longer, and I came around where

they could see me.

"There she is." The general took my hand and kissed it lightly after straightening up and clicking his heels together. "I hear music. You kids go dance. Then you will always be able to tell your kids that you danced at the White House." He placed my hand in Jack's. "I had better go and find my better-half, so she can brag about dancing at the White House, too. Nice talking with you, Staff Sergeant." With that said, he was gone.

Jack smiled at me. "I do believe that I am here with the prettiest girl. Since I have a direct order from a general, I guess we will just have to dance."

Dance we did! For the rest of the night!

Day 7 - Morning

I dreamed that night of all the good things: the grand dinner party, the glitter and pomp of the White House, and most of all of dancing with Jack. I had met the President of the United States and the First Lady. I had been given a tour of the White House, even upstairs to places where visitors aren't usually allowed. No, it wasn't a dream. I was awake, and it had all really happened! I remembered making love to Jack most of the night.

Jack was not in bed. I looked over at the other bed and it was also empty. I sat up and saw that he was seated by the window. He sat in one chair with the other pulled close enough to rest his feet on with his knees up. The position looked uncomfortable. He was wearing only his pants, and a pair of worn binoculars hung from his neck. He raised them slowly and looked through the angled gap in the curtains that he had strategically arranged.

"What are you doing?" I asked.

"Just looking," he replied softly.

"Looking at what?" All of my sleepiness was gone.

"I guess you haven't noticed, but we have been attracting attention. I've been on the watch ever since we got chased in Georgetown the other evening. We've picked up a tail. I wasn't sure at first, but then I saw the same guys twice. Last night they followed us and peeled off when we got to the White House. The same car was parked across the street when we came back last night. This morning there's a man and a woman in that same car."

"Can I look?"

He handed me the binoculars. I reached for the curtain, but he gently blocked my hand. "No need to let them know that we're on to them. Just look at an angle, using one eye, for a brown Rambler station wagon."

I looked carefully. There was a brown station wagon with two people inside. One of them could be a woman. I could not make out any other details, so I asked, "What do we do?"

"Well, I think I'll call room service. I could use a cup of coffee."

I hit him playfully. "Is that all you can think of, your comforts?"

"Oh, with the proper stimulation I could have other ideas." I rubbed him through his pants, and he reached inside my shirt and lightly touched my flesh.

We came together with passion. An hour later as I came out of the shower, Jack was in the process of paying the waiter. I waited until the door had closed before I made an entrance. I had on a robe, and Jack had slipped on his pants again. He had ordered breakfast for us. Just sitting there with nothing on underneath my robe felt naughty, but a good naughty. It couldn't be bad if I was with someone I loved. At first we ate in silence, but I had questions and could not resist.

"So what does one do to win the Medal of Honor?"

Jack just looked at me for several long moments; I felt like a bug under a microscope. He was a little red, and I realized he was embarrassed.

"There are certain things that are not discussed in polite company," he finally responded.

"I just thought since we know each other so well, that

you might tell me. I've never known a hero before."

"Do you ask your parents about their sex lives?" Now it was my turn to be embarrassed. He continued this line of inquiry, "You do know your parents have sex?"

"Sorry, I didn't realize it was such a touchy subject."

"Well, it is. And for your future information, there are no heroes. Heroes are stories or myths. No one person can live up to that. There are only scared men who find themselves in impossible situations, who are just lucky. Lucky that they don't crack up, and that they happen to do the right thing."

We continued eating in silence. I had broken the mood, or so I thought. When Jack finished eating, he just looked at me.

"What are you looking at?"

"You. You know you are beautiful."

"Oh sure. Sitting here in a bathrobe, no makeup, and my hair everywhere. I know I'm too skinny, my breasts are too small, and besides that, I have a smart mouth."

He shook his head. "You were stunning last night, but this morning you are beautiful. I guess I just realized that I love you. What a combination: the leatherneck and the protester."

I stood and walked around to him and sat in his lap. We kissed.

"You make me feel beautiful, even though I know the truth. Okay, I'll admit I am attracted to you," I teased. "And, I think that I love you too," I replied more seriously.

"So when do we get married?" He was earnest and direct.

"Married?"

"Yes, married. That's what two people who are in love do."

"That's the old fashioned answer. We're at the dawning of Aquarius. Marriage is not the only thing that must result from love. Let's just enjoy the moment."

"Oh, I want to enjoy the moment, but this moment won't last forever. The war will be over someday, and I realize now that I want more. That more, includes you."

I kissed him again. "Thanks Jack. It's great to be really wanted, but I have plans, too. I really never think about going down the same trail as my parents. My dad works long hours and comes home late. I guess you could say I never really see him. My mother has lots of really nice things, yet she drinks. That cannot be my future."

"At least you have parents. No matter how bad you think they are, it's better than having none at all. You have choices; you don't have to repeat the mistakes your mother made." He was smiling, almost making fun of me.

"Let's drop the subject. I need to think about it. We will come back to it later." He nodded his agreement, but I could tell the question was not really resolved in his mind, so I changed the subject. "By the way, I have fulfilled my part of the bargain. You owe me."

"I owe you?"

"Yes. One bus ticket for one special date."

"You're leaving?"

"Maybe."

"Okay, we will get your ticket this morning." He started to stand, but I grabbed the arm of the chair and held on. "Not so fast. I just wanted to be sure that you would do what you said you would."

"I always keep my word," he replied solemnly.

"So I have discovered. It is an unusual trait in today's world. But if I have my ticket, I can stay or leave of my own free will. Do you have something in mind for today? A reason for me to stay?"

"I'm sure we can find something to do. After all, I still have a week."

There was a knock at the door. I jumped up and ran for the bathroom and eased the door almost shut. Jack stood by the room door. "Who's there?" He called out, loud enough to be heard through the door.

"Police!" Came the reply. "To see Sergeant Jakes and Miss Marks."

Two officers entered our room as I closed the door to the bathroom. I could hear muffled voices through the door as I tossed off the robe and got dressed as quickly as possible. Fortunately, I was still using the bathroom as a laundry and had washed my dress and underclothes. I had just gotten my dress over my head when there was a tapping at the door.

Jack called through the door, "Are you decent? The gents out here want you to join us."

"Be right there. I called out as I hastily brushed my hair. I smoothed out my dress then went out. They were all standing.

The black officer held up his badge in a flip folder with his ID. "Miss Marks, I'm Detective Thomas." He pointed to his partner. "This is Detective Smith. We are investigating a murder."

"Murder?" My voice croaked.

"Yes, the murder of one Bruce A. Norton."

"Bruce?" I was aghast.

"May I assume from your reaction that you know the gentleman?"

"Yes." I tried to regain control of myself, but my voice quavered. "He was our faculty advisor for this trip to Washington."

Jack interrupted and asked, "What led you to want to question us?"

If the question bothered Detective Thomas, he did not show it. Cops like to ask questions, not answer them.

"First of all, the dead man had Miss Marks' wallet on him as well as his own. I just put two and two together after we had spoken at the precinct, and I came to the conclusion that this was the man who had assaulted Miss Marks."

It dawned on me that Jack had spoken with this man before. He must be the detective Jack had told me about. I was a little stunned, but I tried to control the anger in my voice. "You already know about that, Detective?"

"Yes, and it seemed prudent, in light of recent events, to speak with you."

Detective Thomas pulled a Polaroid picture from his pocket and showed it first to Jack, then to me. I was even more shocked. I had seen my grandfather after he had died, but that had been at the funeral home after he had been prepared. Bruce was swollen and his features distorted. I could not speak. I only managed to nod yes.

Jack spoke offhandedly, "That's him; he never looked so

good. It looks like you fished him out as a floater."

"Yes, he was found at the naval yard in the Anacosta River. The naval diving school is right there by the presidential yacht, Sequoia. Actually, he had not become a floater yet; he hadn't been in the water that long. One of the student divers found him underwater while working on a school project. We figured that he probably went off at the 11th Street Bridge on Thursday night."

"I'll bet that young sailor was real happy to find old Bruce there." Jack's flippant comment about something so gruesome made me cringe. "So, what makes you think he was not a suicide?"

Detective Thomas opened his little notebook. He didn't really look at the page before replying, "The coroner says there was no water in his lungs, which would have been the case had he jumped and drowned. Of course the other clue was that a gun case loaded with rocks was handcuffed to his arm. That's probably what kept him from drifting too far down stream. The doc also made another significant find: His neck was broken before he went in the water."

"Okay, I understand that he was killed, and I'm sure that you two are not here to return Pam's wallet. So why talk to us? We haven't seen this clown since the night he assaulted Pam."

Detective Smith cleared his throat before speaking; he had our attention. "The doc seems to think that whoever broke Mr. Norton's neck was a professional. I pulled your service record, or at least what I could get. You're an expert in martial arts, a black belt in Akido, I believe. You certainly don't seem to mind killing, and you had an altercation with Mr. Norton over your girlfriend. Putting two and two together gives you motive, ability, and as you two have been wandering around sightseeing, opportunity seems to be there, too. You are the logical one to talk with and ask some very direct questions."

Silence greeted the accusation. I looked at Jack; the muscles in his neck were flexing, but when he spoke there was no indication in his voice of the anger that was evident to me. "First, Sir, Akido is a defensive art. I believe you are confusing it with karate, which is an attack method of fighting that involves breaking arms and necks. Of course there are plenty of methods taught in basic marine training that include hand-to-hand combat. Bruce was a big uncoordinated lout who certainly deserved to be tossed in the slammer after someone put some lumps on his head. But, no matter how big a jerk he was, I would not have killed him except in self-defense. As for opportunity, Pam and I have been together almost continuously since his assault on her. And, she was not my girlfriend when that occurred."

"Okay," Detective Thomas interjected, "We had to ask. In any case, we were hoping that you two could give us some idea of where to look. Miss Marks, did you not come to Washington with Mr. Norton?"

"Sure," my voice squeaked, "but as Jack says, we have not seen him since the night he assaulted me. The other kids know him better. Ask them. They are probably all over at the White House protesting the war."

"Jack here had already told me where the bus was. It's not there anymore. I sent someone over to talk with the protesters, and your particular group has not been around for a few days."

A sharp chill went through me. Could something have

happened to Betty and the others?

"Is that why you guys set up a stakeout on us?" From the tone of his voice, Jack was obviously irritated.

"There is no stakeout. We're just asking questions." Detective Thomas seemed insulted.

"Brown Rambler out front," Jack replied in a flat statement.

Smith went over to the window and looked out without moving the drape. "I don't see a Rambler."

Jack took two long steps over to the window and looked out. "It's gone now. Be assured it was there when we got up this morning."

"I believe you," Smith responded, but his voice was thick with doubt. "We will look into it."

"I'm sorry we couldn't be more helpful," I told Detective Thomas.

He reached into his shirt pocket and produced a business card. "My numbers are on there. If either of you think of anything that might help, please call. If we are out, we'll call back as soon as possible."

I took the card. It was embossed with the crest of the Metropolitan Police, his name, and two phone numbers. "Okay."

The two shook hands with Jack and nodded politely to me on their way out. When the door shut I spoke, "Those pigs! They have a lot of nerve accusing us."

Jack hesitated before replying. I realized that he was listening at the door to be sure they had left. "They have a tough job. Don't be so hard on them."

"Why didn't you tell them what happened the night before last?"

"They didn't believe us about the Rambler; they probably wouldn't believe us about the car in the alley. We have to be real careful. They would hang old Brucie's murder on us in a heartbeat! Case closed. We are way too convenient and certainly seem to have a motive. Our alibi is each other. That's crap, and they know it."

Now I was really starting to get frightened. I hugged myself close to hide my shivers. "What do we do?"

"We are good citizens, and this is still a free country. We can poke around and check things out."

"Where do we start?"

"The bus."

"He said the bus was gone."

"Remember, you said those kids protesting would not talk to the cops. But they might talk with another protester, like you."

Day 7 - Afternoon

It was a long afternoon. We worked our way along the Mall speaking with each group of protesters. It did not take long to confirm what the police had told us. The bus I had come on was gone, and so were the kids from my university. There were still a lot of different groups protesting various things–so much unrest. There were several different factions of war protesters from other colleges. There were also several other groups: black protestors concerned with civil rights, women's rights protesters, and a new group of environmental protesters opposed to automobiles and concerned with global cooling.

At first Jack stayed with me, but it soon became apparent that he was a problem. His short hair and neat clothing made him look too much like a cop.

"We aren't doing any good here. Let's go down to the White House," I suggested.

"No." Jack was adamant. "I'm bad enough, but even you are too tidy for these people. Let's face it; we stand out like a skunk at a wedding."

Then it hit me. "Let's go shopping." I led the way back across the Mall into the downtown shopping district. We returned to the store where Jack had bought my new wardrobe just days before. I walked boldly down the aisles and finally halted all the way in the back by the wigs.

"You don't need a wig," Jack tossed out. "I like your hair just fine the way it is."

"I don't need a wig, but you do." I picked up a nice dark one which was a close color-match for his hair. "Try this."

"You're not getting one of those things on me!" Jack protested.

"Yes I am." I led him by the hand to the dressing rooms, and we slipped into one of them together. I flopped it onto his head. "Yes, this will work just fine."

He was scowling something awful. "How much does this damn thing cost?"

I looked at the tag, "Fourteen dollars and ninety-five cents."

"That's outrageous!"

Thirty minutes later we had the wig in a bag and were at a second-hand clothing store. I did feel a little uncomfortable in there. I'm not sure if it was because we were the only white people in the store, or if it was because I had never shopped in such a place. After several passes through the racks, we had some clothing that was more hip and much more like the clothes worn by the protesting kids. Jack called them hippie-clothes. But he didn't look bad in bell-bottoms and a flowered shirt.

As we started out, Jack stopped me. "The Rambler's back." We stepped back inside the store and peered out through a rack of clothes. "You got a pen?"

"No, but I'll get one." I went back to the counter, smiled nicely at the lady, and asked to borrow her pen and a piece of scrap paper. I carefully wrote down the license number as Jack read it off. We returned the pen and went out the back way.

Ten minutes later we were back at the hotel, and Jack took a moment to check the shopping bags with the bellhop.

By the time we got back to the area near the White House, there was hardly anyone there. "What gives?" Jack asked.

I explained that most activity ended once the evening news started.

"You mean all this is just for show?" Jack was shocked.

"Good PR is important for any movement. You can't tell me the marines don't try to put out the best PR they can."

"Sure they do," he grinned. "Why do you think they've been parading me all around town? It's all for show too."

"Let's go down to the end of the Mall by the tidal basin. A lot of the kids are staying there."

"I'm surprised that they don't arrest them for vagrancy."

"I heard that they tried that for a while during the civil rights protests, but some smart lawyers got the practice stopped."

"It's probably just as well. It's always been a lousy practice."

I was out of breath by the time we got to the basin area. It had been a fair stretch of our legs. We had done quite a bit of walking today, but Jack seemed oblivious to the effort.

"All this walking sure doesn't seem to bother you." I observed.

"You have to remember that we do a lot of walking in the corps, and here I don't have to carry a full field pack and ammo."

"I guess I just don't have the right attitude."

There were four buses in the area, and maybe thirty or forty kids. We started with the first group. I explained that I was looking for my friends in a green chartered bus from the University of Wisconsin. No luck. We moved from group to group. Finally, at the fourth group, someone said that a Jenny was dating one of the guys from the green bus. She wasn't there, but she was expected back any time. She had gone shopping after they stopped protesting. We were invited to have dinner. We didn't really want any dinner, but it seemed to be the best way to hang around.

After dinner one of the guys lit a joint and passed it around. I took a cautious drag when it was my turn. I was curious to see what Jack would do. He took the joint and passed it on without taking a drag.

"Hey, man," one of the guys called out, "That's good shit! You too good to smoke our shit? Or maybe you're a narc."

"No way," Jack protested. "Appreciate the offer, but

can't; got asthma. Tried it once and all it got me was a trip to the hospital and a 4-F classification."

"Sorry," came the reply, "Can't be too careful nowadays."

About that time we were interrupted by the arrival of five girls laden with shopping bags. "Hi Jenny," another girl called out, her speech slurred from the effects of the grass. "These guys want to see you about Jerry."

"What about Jerry?"

The girl had straight, long blond hair all the way down to her waist and wore wire frame glasses. She had on an ankle-length white linen dress that was so thin all of her curves were plainly visible. She was quite obviously not wearing a bra. I would have been cold in a dress like that, since it was late now and almost dark.

I stood and walked toward her. "I'm not just looking for Jerry. I'm looking for the bus he was on."

"They must have gone, 'cause they haven't been around since before the weekend."

I could tell that something was troubling her. "Can we talk for a few minutes? Privately?" I asked.

She paused to think. "Come on, I've got to put my things away."

I followed her onto the bus. It was pretty much the same set-up as the bus I had come on. The students lived on or camped around the bus, while the organizers had a room somewhere nearby. She stopped halfway down the aisle and tossed her bag into the overhead bin.

"I can't tell you much. Jerry and I hung around together

for a few days. We marched together, got drunk, had some laughs, and then he was gone."

"I came on that bus. It wasn't scheduled to go back until Friday."

"I don't know anything about that. He did talk about some people who were missing. Some girl who was a thief ran off, then a teacher went missing. You wouldn't happen to be the thief-girl?"

This was not going to be easy. "No, I'm not a thief. I'm a girl who escaped an attempted rape. Now I'm worried about my friends."

"There was something wrong with that bunch," Jenny commented. "Jerry and I spent more time over here than over there. A couple of the guys that hung around that bus gave me the creeps. They drove a shitty Merc. They came back one day with it all busted up on the right side and couldn't even open the door. Next day they had a Rambler, a big Ambassador. I sure thought that Jerry would have said goodbye, or at least gotten my number and address."

"Thanks. I guess I'll have to get a Greyhound back to campus."

"Sorry I couldn't be more help. Did they take off with all your stuff?" She was looking at the rags that I was wearing.

"Yes, but it's okay. I'll get by."

Day 8 - Morning

We were up early the next morning and eager to find out if the watchers were back. We were not disappointed. The Rambler was back in position. The night before, Jack had carefully positioned a chair to hold back the drape so we could observe the street below from an angle that kept us in the shadows. I kept watch while Jack was dressing.

The car was extremely dirty, but it appeared to be a tan color. The angle of the windows prevented a clear view of the people inside, but there were obviously two of them in the front seat. I tried to memorize every detail of the car, from the white sidewall tires to the dents. The radio antenna was bent, there was a dent on the front left fender, and the back left window was cracked.

Jack came out and laced up a pair of sneakers. I had never seen him wear anything but the same pair of loafers. "Time to do a little recon."

"Recon?" I didn't know what he meant.

"Recon. Scouting around to you," he replied, donning his wig. "Give me a fifteen minute head start then go down to the coffee shop in your pink dress. Sit outside where they can see you. Have a cup of coffee and get one to go for me. I'll meet you back up here in thirty minutes."

"I'm not sure about this. Is it necessary? Maybe we should call the detectives."

"Let's wait and talk with them when we have something to tell them." Jack seemed confident, and it was contagious.

"Okay," I agreed.

So I followed orders. That is the best way to describe it.

Somehow it seemed the natural thing to do. I went directly to the coffee shop and sat exactly as instructed. Oh, how badly I wanted to look at the Rambler, but I knew I dared not. I bought a paper and sat with two cups of coffee for exactly thirty minutes. I tried to read the paper, but that was an impossible task. I just looked at several headlines. The price of gold–more battles in Vietnam–the rest was a blur. At the end of thirty minutes I stood and asked the waitress for some paper cups and left with two coffees to go.

I went up to the room as fast as possible. Jack was already there talking on the phone. "Okay," he said into the receiver. He looked directly at me while holding up one finger in the classic 'wait-a-moment' gesture. "We'll be by shortly. Thanks very much."

As the phone settled into the cradle, I couldn't wait any longer. "What did you find out?"

"I got close enough to the Rambler to hear them talking. Their names are Tony and Bill, and they are not real happy about their assignment."

"Was that the police on the phone?"

"No, that was the garage. Gunny's car is fixed, so we will have wheels again."

"Aren't we going to the police about Tony and Bill?"

"We really don't know what they're up to, besides no good. We've made progress, but not enough to satisfy Detective Thomas."

"So, what do we do now?" He had me confused.

"We turn the tables on the hunters."

"I don't understand."

"The hunters become the hunted. We'll follow them. Those two are just foot soldiers. They have to report to someone. Get your jeans on, girl! There may be some running involved."

I started unbuttoning my dress as he continued to talk.

"Let's hurry. They may get tired of waiting, and we need to get the car."

I started pulling on some jeans we had picked up. "How do we get out? They are parked where they can see the lobby and both entrances to the hotel." I had noticed during my time at the coffee shop that the front windows of the hotel afforded a view of the elevators, front desk, and all entrances. They had obviously parked in a position to take advantage of the hotel's structure.

Jack was changing into his hippie-clothes. "Never saw a place yet that didn't have other exits. I left through the basement and went out through the delivery area in the back alley. We can go out that way." He pulled on his wig. "Ready?"

I was buttoning my blouse. "Ready."

We took the elevator to the second floor and used the stairs to go on down to the basement. Once in the back alley we crossed over and went through the rear entrance of a store, then out its front entrance and onto the street. There was another hotel across the street with a line of cabs waiting. Jack let another couple have the first cab and we took the second. Jack asked the cab driver to take us to the Lincoln Memorial. We made several turns as Jack watched behind us to be sure that we were not being followed. He asked the driver to circle the monument a couple of times so we could look at it from all sides, but we weren't really looking at the monument. Jack was watching the traffic, and I was watching for the Rambler, too.

Jack handed the cabbie an address, and we went to a body shop in the southeast area by the Navy Yard. It was a very run down area of the city.

"Look there." The cab driver pointed to a large brick building that must have been twelve to fifteen stories tall. "Less than five years old and already needs to be torn down. Built for the welfare people, and it has already been condemned. They have destroyed the place."

I could see plainly that there were not very many unbroken windows left, but the brick looked fairly new. When we turned the corner I saw the front of the building, and it was obvious that there had been a fire. The doorways and windows on the ground floor were covered with plywood. The front walkways and yards were heaped with trash and furniture. There was nothing there I would ever want in any home of mine. Jack and I said nothing. I just gripped his hand.

The cab driver was not finished. "When d'you figure the government is going to learn that you just can't give a home to folks who did not earn it? All you create is poor people who resent the government. Folks need to earn something to take pride in it."

Jack finally spoke, "Guess we are seeing our modern democracy at work."

The cab driver lit a cigarette. "Guess so, but it still seems to be a waste of taxpayers' money. Here we are, A-1 Auto. That'll be three-fifty, Mac. Need me to wait?"

Jack handed him four dollars. "Keep the change. No need to wait; we are picking up our wheels."

"Don't stick around this area, especially after dark. Matter of fact, I wouldn't have brought you down here after dark." The cabbie seemed anxious to leave.

We went up to the small shabby office and a black man greeted Jack. "She is all ready to go." As he handed Jack the key he pointed out to the fence. "I'll open the gate when you're ready."

I was surprised to see that the car was now two-tone. The upper-half, roof, and panels were still cream, but the lower-half was lime green. When we rolled out of the gate there was no traffic. Jack turned right and then made a series of turns, weaving back and forth.

"I hope your friend doesn't mind a different color on his car."

"Figured it was best not to paint it the same color. They were painting one side anyway, and it was only an extra twenty-five dollars to have both sides painted. It cost seventy-five for the repairs. Never met a marine yet that didn't like green."

I was a bit turned around, but Jack wasn't. He drove back toward the hotel, turned up an alley and parked next to a dumpster. From there we could see the trunk of the Rambler. Jack switched off the engine. He got out and walked to the corner, peeked around it, then came back.

"They are still there," he said as he climbed back into the car.

We sat and waited.

Day 8 - Afternoon

It was exactly three o'clock when the Rambler started its engine. Jack started the Ford and we eased forward a little.

When the Rambler pulled out into traffic, we followed. Jack stayed back two or three car lengths, following at a discreet distance. The two in the car were apparently unaware we were following. Jack was good at this.

"Have you ever done this before?" I asked idly.

"Nope."

"Did you learn this in the marines?"

"No, just from watching TV and reading PI stories. Doesn't seem real hard." The Rambler sped through an intersection and we got caught at a red light. "So much for not real hard. Guess we are going to lose them after all." Halfway down the block the Rambler hit the brakes and turned left.

We followed, but they were gone. Luckily, it was obvious where they had gone: into a warehouse with several roll-up doors. There was a puddle and wet tire tracks by the door showing where the Rambler had driven in.

"Looks like you got lucky," I teased Jack.

"It's always better to be lucky than good." He grinned the wide smile I had come to enjoy. "However, it's even better to be some of each."

The warehouse seemed to take up most of the block. Jack drove past it and down to the corner where he turned left and pulled up to the curb. We walked to the alley, then went behind the building. It seemed to be an old manufacturing plant badly in need of repair. There was trash and debris in the alley, and by the looks of it, the trash had been there for a long time. I tried to look through some of the lower windows, but they were so dirty it was almost impossible to see inside. What I could see looked mostly empty and deserted. We got to the section where the loading docks were, and Jack hopped up onto the four-foot platform with ease. He offered his hand and pulled me up. The windows were the old safety type with wire reinforcement for durability. It would be hard to break in, as was indicated by signs of previously failed attempts. All of the doors were metal and looked real sturdy. I ducked when I saw movement in the interior.

Jack had already ducked down and was on the move. Glancing around, I saw a small hole that had once allowed a wire to pass through the wall. It took a moment to focus, but then I could see inside through the hole. Two cars were parked in the big room next to an old wooden desk. One of the men was talking on the phone, but I couldn't hear. Then a small gasp escaped my lips; parked along the far wall was the bus that I had come to Washington in! I jerked back. Jack was fifteen feet away from me listening at a mail slot. When I looked back through the hole, the men were looking in my direction. They had heard me.

I looked at Jack, and he motioned for me to move toward the edge of the loading dock. We moved at the same time, and at the edge I didn't hesitate – I jumped. Jack came to me in a crouching run. We moved back another ten feet to where a rickety staircase provided access to the dock. We ducked under it and found a small opening in the concrete. Ordinarily I would never enter such a space, but the door above creaked open, and I ducked in. Jack squeezed in after me.

We could hear footsteps above us, and a voice rumbled, "You're getting as bad as an old lady. There's no one here."

"I heard something," the other voice replied defiantly.

"Probably rats," the first voice sounded disgusted. Just then I could hear the far-away ringing of a phone. "Shit! She's calling back and we're out here on a wild goose chase. Get your ass back inside and bolt the door!" As the phone rang again we could hear the thumping of a big man hustling toward the sound.

A cigarette butt went flying past us down into the alley. The phone had stopped ringing. Long moments later we heard the door creak shut and the grating noise of a bolt sliding into place. I let my breath out and realized my knees were in pain from my cramped position. Jack eased forward and helped me from the hole. I started to speak, but he held his finger to his lips. We stayed under the stairs for a couple of minutes, and then Jack motioned for me to stay. He went back down the loading dock toward our car for twenty or thirty feet, then jumped up and moved out of sight. I passed the time rubbing some life back into my abused legs. I was a little startled when Jack jumped back down beside me.

He whispered in my ear, "They're back away from the windows. Come on, and be careful." He jumped up, offered me his hand, and pulled me up with ease. We moved back along the wall and took up our previous positions, with Jack listening at the mail slot and me peeking.

The bigger man was arguing on the phone while the little guy leaned on the rickety desk. Finally, the big man slammed down the receiver. The men talked briefly, then the big man got into the Rambler and started the car. The little guy opened the roll-up door and held it while the Rambler pulled out, and then he pulled on the chain and the big door slid down. He got in on the passenger side of the car and they pulled away.

I stood up and threw my arms around Jack's neck. "I thought we were goners for sure."

"Just keep thinking that way."

"What?"

"I said, just keep thinking that way. That man was trying to explain why they haven't gotten rid of us yet. From his side of the conversation, I can only conclude that since they haven't managed to scare us off, they have orders to get rid of us permanently."

"Kill us?"

"I think so."

"Do you think they killed the kids I came with? The bus that's in there is the one I came on."

"So I gathered from your reaction. No, I don't think they killed the kids. There has to be some other explanation."

"I'm sorry about making noise. What do we do now?"

"Let's see if we can find some way inside."

Jack jumped off the loading dock and walked across the alley, looking the building over from a distance. He jumped back up and said, "Wait here, I'll be right back."

There is something to be said for agility. Jack went up the drain pipe next to the dock like a monkey, hand over hand. When he reached the overhang, he gracefully swung up and pulled himself onto the roof. I could hear his footsteps crunch on the gravel roof, then all was quiet, and I was left alone with my thoughts. I looked down and could see dirt on my blouse. I brushed it off as best as I could. Then I unconsciously ran my hands through my hair and they came away with cobwebs. I worked hard not to think of anything else but getting the webs out of my hair.

It could not have been more than a few minutes when the bolt on the door was retracted. Jack swung the door open.

"Your ladyship, the way is clear for you to step into the lion's den."

I remember the smell: dank and musty. We could clearly see the trail in the dusty floor where the men had walked. We walked carefully in their trail, careful not to make any new paths, straight to the bus. The door stood open like a foreboding cave. I hesitated. Could they have harmed my friends? Jack was right behind me, and I gathered strength from him and moved on. I climbed up the first step, then the second, and I was in. My eyes had to adjust. The bus looked empty, but I had to know for sure. Step-by-step I moved down the aisle, expecting to see a body at any time. I made it all the way to the back. Thank God! No bodies. The bus was empty.

I turned around and bumped into Jack. I couldn't help it; all I could do was hug him in sheer relief. He patted my back. "Don't worry; we will figure this out. The best evidence you have that they have not done the unthinkable is the fact that there is no evidence of violence here."

I made no reply as I held on to him. When I looked up I saw the open overhead bins, and the edge of a familiar shape came into focus. I released Jack and stepped past him. "Look," I said, "They left my bag." It was not big, but it was the same ratty-brown bag that had been in my family for years. Mother had given it to me when I'd left for college. I grabbed the handle and pulled it down. It was heavier than it had been, and I was surprised by its weight. I almost dropped it.

I put it on the seat and unsnapped the latches on each side. I opened it expecting to see my clothes, but the suitcase contained weird square-shaped objects with a bunch of wires and three clocks. I stood there dumbfounded, looking into my suitcase. "What the hell…?"

Jack pushed up against me. "Be very careful." He had a hard edge to his voice.

"What is it?"

"A bomb," he said very matter-of-factly. "Looks like C-4 rigged with fulminate of mercury caps and a timing device. Triple backup."

"How big?"

"Big or small, we sure wouldn't be around to give any details if this thing went off with us in here. Go on! Just leave me! I'll pull its fangs."

He pushed me gently. I have to admit it did not take much to get me going. I wanted to put as much distance between myself and that suitcase as possible. When I got to the door he called out to me, "Wait below the loading dock, and remember to stay in the dust path. If this goes off just get to the car and drive away."

I went back to the old rusted metal door and eased it open. Its creaking noise seemed way too loud now. I did as instructed and went back into the small opening below the stairs. I didn't give the cobwebs even a moment of thought. I could only guess that Jack figured that this was a safe area if anything went wrong. Then it dawned on me that he'd told me to drive off, but he had been driving, and he had the keys! The door creaked and then the bolt slid shut. I came out of my hole and looked up at the loading dock. My heart dropped – my suitcase sat all alone. Then I heard Jack's footsteps on the roof above. He swung over the edge and gracefully dropped down onto the dock.

"What in the hell…?" I pointed to the suitcase.

"Don't worry; I pulled the caps out. It's safe now; just a bunch of wires and plastic."

Jack casually picked up the suitcase and headed down the alley toward the car. He opened the door, scooped the keys off the floorboard, and opened the trunk.

"Very good," he said, pulling a small green box from the trunk. It had faded yellow writing which I could not read. He opened it and dumped out a bunch of tools. Then he reached under his shirt and pulled out a small bundle which appeared to be his tee shirt rolled up with wires sticking out of it. He placed the bundle in the box. As he snapped the latches into place he explained, "This is an old ammo-box. A lot of marines keep them. It's the safest place to store caps separate from the C4. If the caps get too hot they get unstable and can go off. These electric caps have been known to be set off by static. Caps are best stored in a cool place and safely stored away. The people who put that bomb together sure don't care who gets hurt. A bunch of real sick bastards!"

He put the suitcase in the trunk and asked, "Will you hold the caps while I drive? If not, I'll hold 'em while you drive."

"You drive." I reluctantly held out my hand to take the green box.

We got in the car and drove in silence for many blocks.

Finally I asked, "Does any of this make any sense? Why an empty bus full of explosives?"

Jack paused and cleared his throat. "The only thing that makes any sense right now is diversion."

"Diversion?"

"That's right. Someone is going to blow up the bus as a diversion to draw attention away from something else."

"What?"

"I don't know, but I've got bad gut-feeling about all this, and that's not good, cause it usually means something bad is going to happen."

Day 8 - Evening

We made a stop by the Marine Barracks. Jack went in alone with the green box containing the caps while I waited in the car. He returned a few minutes later without the box, and we drove to the train station. I waited again while Jack went inside with my suitcase. Minutes later, he returned empty-handed.

As he slid into the car, he handed me a locker key. "Your suitcase is in locker 299," he said.

"I'm not so sure I want it back."

He grinned at me. "The number is not on the key, and one of us will have to tell the police where it's at."

I shoved the key in my pocket. "Why didn't you leave the explosives with the marines? It would make more sense than leaving them at the train station."

"Actually, I didn't even officially leave the caps with the marines. If I had, I'd have been answering questions and filling out forms for two days, as well as doing some verbal dancing with some squid JAG asshole - officer. I just left the caps in

Gunny's reefer and asked him to keep the can cool for a few days."

"Marijuana?"

He blew out a sigh, "Refrigerator to you."

"And what is a squid JAG asshole?"

"A squid is anyone in the navy. JAG means Judge Advocate General; that's a military lawyer. All lawyers, and navy pukes, by definition, are considered assholes, especially when you are a lowly marine grunt."

"Your friend is taking a big risk. Why would he do that?"

"Actually, Gunny probably would keep the caps for me, but I didn't give him the opportunity to turn me down. I just shoved the box in his freezer and asked him to keep it for me. No one is going to search the Gunny's reefer or question anything that's in there. But this way, on the remote chance they do, he can play dumb honestly."

"What now?" I asked.

Jack reached into his pocket and pulled out a piece of paper he'd taken from a tablet in the warehouse. He had rubbed the flat side of a pencil tip across the page to bring out the impression of what had been written on the page before it. It read: 'Dan's Bar and Grill,' followed by a phone number and address.

"Thought we'd go there for dinner. If those guys show up, we might learn something."

"That's a long shot," I said, thinking aloud. "Sounds like something from an old private eye movie."

"Well, It could be nothing," he replied with a sly grin.

"But on the other hand, we have to eat, so why not check it out?"

Dan's Bar and Grill wasn't one of the better places in Washington. It smelled of old beer and Lysol, mixed with whatever odors accumulate in a bar that's seen lots of smoking and drinking over the years. The building had probably been around since World War I, and this establishment had probably seen its best days during World War II. Now it just looked shabby. It wasn't real big, but it seemed to be doing a brisk business. It had two sections: a bar on one side, and a dining area on the other. There were tables down the center and booths along the wall. It was the local hangout for what Daddy would call blue-collar workers. Most of the patrons looked like they had just come from work at a construction site.

Jack led the way through the dining side to the booth in the far corner. Just as we got there, a frazzled-looking older woman wearing a less-than-clean apron popped out from the back. She had a name tag pinned crookedly to her blouse. An embossing label-gun had been used to write her name: Molly.

"Two for dinner." Jack said, "Can we sit in this booth?"

The woman grinned showing yellow, gapped teeth. She spoke with an Irish accent, "Just help yourselves."

As we slid into the booth across from each other, she shoved worn plastic-covered menus in front of us. The menus had blue typed lettering, like ditto sheets used in schools. These were the first reasonable prices I had seen. A burger with everything, plus fries, was seventy-nine cents. A Coke was twenty cents, and a milk shake was fifty-nine cents. While we glanced at the menus, Molly put two glasses of water on our table.

"Something to drink?" she asked.

"Coke," I replied.

"Coke will be fine," Jack added.

Molly produced a worn tablet and started writing. "Ready to order, or do you need more time with the menu?"

"I'm ready," Jack answered.

"Burger and fries for me." I replied.

"Make that two." Jack added.

"Good choice," she commented. "The cook just cleaned the grill today. Cheese?"

I shook my head no, and Jack did too.

"Not exactly the Flagship." I wasn't sure if Jack was trying to apologize, or what.

"This is just fine," I assured him. "So tell me, what do you expect to find here?"

"I don't know, but if we were in a movie, there would be a mysterious waiter, and the bar would be filled with all kinds of interesting suspects."

"I think the only thing the suspects at this bar have any interest in, is drinking as much beer as possible as quickly as possible."

Jack leaned forward and looked hard at the group at the bar. "Yep, that just about sums it up."

I couldn't help it; I giggled. No matter how bad things seemed, Jack made me feel better.

Molly returned with our Cokes in tall frosty mugs with straws. "You kids from out of town?"

"Yes," I replied. "Just taking in the sights."

"Be careful," she replied, "All them nut cases are down

by the Mall protesting one thing or another. Ain't always safe."

"Don't worry," Jack assured her with a smile. "We're just here for a few days to visit with the president. I'm sure he'll keep us safe."

She glided away, laughing at the strange notion of a couple of kids visiting the president.

Actually, the burgers weren't bad, and the fries were sliced real thin just the way I like them. As we ate, the place started filling up, and the level of noise rose accordingly. By the time we finished eating, the place was almost full. I looked around, and only one table and one booth were empty, and all the bar stools were occupied. We had apparently been pretty hungry, because all conversation between us stopped while we ate. I was lost in thought, trying to make sense of the past few days, but nothing made any sense at all. Molly went by with a tray and managed to drop our bill on our table as she passed.

"Well, well. I'll be," Jack said softly, catching my undivided attention. "Don't look now, but isn't that your girlfriend who just showed up?" He was looking toward the far end of the bar.

Of course, I immediately did exactly what he told me not to do–I turned and craned my neck for a good look. Fortunately, she had her back to us and was busy speaking with a man. I had sense enough to duck back down in the booth as she turned. Aside from a glimpse of his very large nose, I could mostly just see the back of the man's head, so I wasn't sure if I'd seen him before. But, the woman was definitely Betty.

Day 9 - Morning

I woke up feeling wonderful! We had slept in the nude, and Jack was lying up against me. I usually sleep curled up on my side, but I was on my back with Jack's leg across mine and his arm over my chest. I could feel the warmth of his body against mine. I didn't want to move, but after a while I had to. Gently moving him aside, I slid out and padded barefooted into the bathroom.

I looked at myself in the mirror. My face was flushed with excitement. I've always been self-conscious about my body, but everything seemed just right that morning, no doubt due to the night I'd just spent with Jack. But upon closer inspection, I was a bit of a mess. I had no makeup on, was starting to get a pimple, and needed a haircut and a perm. A nice warm shower was in order.

I spent ten luxurious minutes letting the hot water run over me. My thoughts wandered to Betty. She had left the restaurant so suddenly the night before that we had been caught flat-footed. The man she'd been talking to left shortly after she had, while we were still trying to pay our bill. He was a real strange-looking guy. He was middle-aged with rugged, hawkish features. Definitely not her date! He had thick black hair and weird looking eyes that gleamed almost yellow. His most pronounced feature was a long, bent nose. I knew that I would never want to be alone with him.

Later, Jack had been reluctant to discuss the man. When I asked about him, he just grunted and mumbled. When I pressed him, he told me the man was a hunter, and it would be best for me to stay clear of him. Only later did I realize that Jack was one hunter recognizing another.

I turned off the shower, dried off, and reluctantly put on the hotel's white terry cloth robe. Jack dashed into the bathroom as I came out. I was dressed by the time he reappeared. He already had his pants on and took a moment to pull on his shirt and shoes. I was starving. I guess Jack was too. Five minutes later we were ordering breakfast in the coffee shop.

"What now?" I asked.

"This is in no particular order, but we need to figure out what your friend Betty is up to, visit the Smithsonian National Air and Space Museum, and, since our friends in the Rambler are out front again, we need to slip away."

"We need to go to a museum?"

"Why not? We haven't got anything better to do. We can go looking for Betty later." He smiled with a mischievous twinkle in his eyes. "Of course, we could always go back up to the room and fool around for the rest of the day."

"It's not that I would mind fooling around," I could feel myself flushing with embarrassment, "but it's probably better that we go to the museum."

Jack chuckled, and I realized that he wasn't serious, but he had baited me good.

He pulled a bag from under the bed and took out a box. "What have you got?"

"A camera. Figured I could get a few snapshots of my new girl." He held up a Polaroid camera as he broke open a flat pack of film.

"One of those things. My dad has one. Doesn't it only take black and white pictures?"

He shook his head. "No, this is a newer color version. Don't even have to fix the picture afterward." He turned the camera on me and snapped a picture before I could protest. The flash left me seeing spots, as usual.

"Hey, I wasn't ready!" I objected.

He laughed as the camera made a little grinding noise and spit out a blank white picture. He held it by the edges and handed it to me. Something was already starting to show up. I watched as my face and the background of the room steadily came into view. My hair looked terrible, but Jack was elated. "Ain't technology wonderful!" he pronounced. He took back the picture and put it in his shirt pocket.

We slipped out through the back of the hotel and went to the Air and Space Museum. It was just off Fourteenth Street in a series of three or four buildings. The Atlas rockets used in the Mercury Project seemed out of place against the aged red bricks of the weathered buildings. Just inside, there was a model of a newly proposed museum to be constructed off the Mall near the Capitol. The aging floors squeaked as we walked; I guess they did need a new building.

Alan Shepard's capsule, which had carried the first American into space, was on display in the middle of the lobby. After having seen the massive rockets just outside, the capsule looked positively small. There was a suited mannequin lying on the couch, which clearly demonstrated that there was sufficient room for a man inside, but there sure wasn't room for anything else.

Jack commented on exactly what I was thinking, "Now that takes real guts, letting them strap you to the top of a rocket in that tin can."

"I once saw a display in Chicago that showed how big the Niña was. It was one of the ships in which Columbus crossed the Atlantic Ocean. It was pretty small, too."

"Well, four hundred years from now, I hope people realize just what an effort it was to launch a man into space."

"It seems doubtful that we will get to the moon now, since the accident." I pointed to the nearby Apollo memorial plaque. It's there in memory of the three astronauts killed a little more than a year ago in an accident during a test. Gus Grissom, Ed White, and Roger Chaffee died in January of 1967, bringing an apparent end, or at least a long delay, to plans for landing a man on the moon before the end of the decade, as was proposed by President Kennedy.

Jack chuckled that little laugh of his that meant he thought he was so right. "I wouldn't count our astro guys out. They will come ripping back. When they do, those Ruskies will get left in the dust. We might not make it before 1970, but I'd lay even money that we'll make it to the moon before 1975."

"My dad is crazy for all of this space stuff," I told Jack. "He used to get up at three and four in the morning to watch the Project Gemini missions. He really gets off on the space walks and link-ups. He even went out and bought a color TV when we had a perfectly good black and white one. He wanted an even better view of the space shots."

As we looked over the display showing the proposed lunar mission for Apollo, I couldn't help but feel something wonderful about our country's grand achievements. But Jack expressed it best. "I can understand how your dad feels; it's easy to be drawn to the adventure. We're lucky to be able to watch as history is made."

Day 9 - Afternoon

Betty was surprisingly easy to find. We pulled up to our hotel, and there she was just walking out! What was she doing at our hotel? She jumped into a cab, and Jack pulled around to follow it. The cab went toward the southeast section of Washington as if it was going to the Marine Barracks, but then it changed direction and crossed the Eleventh Street Bridge. Jack commented, "This isn't one of the better parts of town."

Looking around, I saw that the area was seedy and run down, not like parts of the city on the other side of the river. Houses in a single block seemed to be linked together. All the people I saw in the area were black. Martin Luther King's dream is that one day all races will live together without differences. But I can't see that happening while areas of racial poverty and segregation like this exist.

"It's hard to look at all this poverty. Thank goodness the president is doing something about it."

Jack was concentrating on following the cab. He made a few smooth maneuvers before replying.

"There have always been poor folks. I don't see how that's going to change."

"It has to," I replied. "Our country is too rich to have poor people."

"It seems to me that the best way to eliminate poverty is to ensure equal opportunity. In other words, to have access to the American capitalist system." He made another series of turns. "But the real question right now is: What is Betty doing in this part of town, and where the hell is she going?"

We blasted through a yellow light and turned right to keep up with the taxi.

"Well one thing's for sure, she's not going to the welfare office to hand out food to the poor," I tossed out this unlikely prospect.

Jack laughed before replying soberly. "You're right about that, and she certainly isn't acting like a college student bent on protesting the war."

Suddenly Jack barked, "Get down!" I put my head in my lap. "They stopped. She's out and paying the cabbie. Didn't want her to recognize you. Now she's walking toward a house. I'm driving past; it's number 1611." I felt the car turn right. "Okay, you can come up for air."

He made a U-turn and parked catty-corner from the address. I adjusted the right-side mirror so I could see the front door of the house. I noticed Jack had done the same with the rear-view mirror.

"What now?"

"We wait."

"How do you know so much about everything? 'We wait'. You always seem to have an answer."

"Well, it might seem that way, but I don't always have the answer. One of the key things the corps teaches is leadership. A good leader should always be positive and should always have an answer. Indecision is a cancer of leadership. People who are unsure of themselves shouldn't be in charge."

"Does that mean you are the leader of our little effort here?"

"No, in this particular case I'm just your partner. I'm just as curious as you are. What we're doing is no different from hunting. Since I've done more hunting than you have, I have a better idea of what comes next. You see, there is a time to follow the trail, a time to wait, and a time to shoot. Right now seems like a good time to wait."

"Okay, that makes sense. I like 'partners'."

"So do I. So, what do you really know about your friend Betty?"

"Not a whole lot. We had a couple of classes together: political science and history. She's a pistol in class, always arguing with professors about one thing or another."

"So, based on your observations of her arguments and your conversations with her, who is she?"

I had to think before answering. "Well, she admires Karl Marx, and she hates corporations. In fact, that's where we really differ. When she found out that my dad owned a company and employed other people, she told me he was part of an evil system. After that, it was a subject we avoided."

"Interesting."

"Interesting? What does that mean?"

"It means interesting. Has it occurred to you that she might be a communist? People who admire Karl Marx just might be against the United States."

"Are you implying that anyone who protests the war is a communist?"

"I don't think that's what I said. We're discussing a specific individual, Karl Marx, not an entire movement."

Jack suddenly sat up and adjusted his mirror, then looked

over his shoulder. "Look at this guy," he hissed. I turned and looked. Jack pushed my head down until just my eyes were above the seat. The tall, big-nosed man from the bar had just come out of the house. Jack ducked as the man looked up and down the street before briskly walking to an old, beat-up black Dodge. He got in and made a quick U-turn away from us. Jack started the engine and made his own U-turn.

As we turned to follow the Dodge, Betty came out of the house. As it was obvious that she had seen us, Jack stopped. Even though his head was turned away from me, I could almost see his grin as he spoke with her. "Need a lift?"

She ignored Jack, speaking directly to me. "I see you are still with this jerk. Yes, I believe I will take a ride."

She opened the back door and slid into the car. Jack was already putting the car in gear and moving forward. I turned to talk to her just in time to see her press the barrel of a small revolver into Jack's neck. Jack stiffened and was silent.

"What the hell. . . ?"

Betty cut me off mid-sentence. "Just drive!" she commanded, speaking to Jack. Her voice was ragged and different. "So, is this jerk a pig?"

Jack picked up speed, smoothly shifting gears. "No, he's just a marine who saved me from Bruce."

"You're still sticking to that story? He looks like an FBI pig." She twisted the gun up behind Jack's ear.

"Jakes, Jackson P., 25678441, Staff Sergeant USMC."

Betty's face went blank. It was obvious she did not understand.

"He's giving you his name, rank, and serial number,

since you are holding us prisoner."

"Turn left at the next street," Betty snapped. Jack slowed and signaled with his arm out the window. "Hand me his wallet," Betty demanded.

Jack carried his wallet in his left rear pocket, so he eased forward to give me access. I had to almost hug him to get to it. I could not hold back as I handed her his wallet. "So now you are just a common thief!"

"You know nothing!" She grabbed the wallet with her free hand and flipped through the view envelopes. She stopped and stared at a green card. "So, you are military. Well, you may not be a pig, but you're still a jerk."

"I told you he wasn't a cop!"

She threw the wallet at my face. I ducked and it glanced off my forehead and landed on the floorboard at my feet. It hurt, but I didn't let on. I didn't want to give her the satisfaction.

Betty kept the gun pressed to Jack's head and continued to give him directions. She was apparently very familiar with the city.

We soon found ourselves back at the warehouse where the bus was hidden. Betty ordered Jack to pull up to the door and blow the horn twice, then once. The door rolled up and Jack pulled the car inside. One of the men who'd been trailing us in the Rambler was working the door's chain.

Betty was out of the car in a flash and opened the left door with one hand while continuing to hold the gun on us. "Come on out you two, this side only." She backed away to give us room. "See, you two lunk heads, it's not so hard to catch two kids."

I had picked Jack's wallet up from the floorboard and still

had it in my hand. I managed to slip it into my pocket as I got out of the car. Betty gestured with her gun for us to move away from the car and into the open area of the warehouse. The bus still sat where it had been, and the Rambler was parked behind it.

"What happened to all the other kids from my school?" I asked, afraid to hear the answer, but needing to know.

"Questions. Always questions. Now is not the time for you to ask questions. Now is the time for you to answer mine. What did you two do with the suitcase you took from the bus?"

"What suitcase?" Jack spoke for the first time.

"So, you want to play dumb? I know it's not in your hotel room." She paused to let that sink in. "I searched it this morning after you left. Did you really think we would not notice when you left the hotel?"

Jack said nothing, so neither did I.

"So, that's the way you want it?" Betty nodded to one of her men and said, "Search the car."

"There is no suitcase in the car." Jack insisted.

Betty's man ignored Jack and began searching our car. We were facing away from it, but could hear its doors opening and the jingle of keys as the trunk was unlocked.

"Nothing here," a voice called out.

"Go over to the table one at a time, and empty your pockets." Betty ordered.

We each stepped over to a small table and did as we were told. The man who had been searching our car walked over with my purse in his hand and tossed it onto the table. Betty ordered her men to search us as she began going through our possessions.

One of the men produced a big ugly revolver and covered us while the other moved in to search us.

"Hands up! Lock your fingers behind your head!"

He frisked Jack first, going over him completely. He stepped back and said, "He's clean."

I was next. It was frightening and humiliating. He took his time feeling my breasts before finally getting around to checking my pockets. I could tell that Jack was fuming with anger, but he kept his cool. The man reached into my front pocket and fished out the key to the train-station locker. All the while, he kept his body pressed up against mine, making sure I could feel him.

"Looks like she held out on us." He gave Betty the key.

"Where is the locker, and what is its number?" she demanded of me.

I just looked at her. I'd never been so angry in all my life! I felt so helpless in the face of indignity. I was almost insensible with fear. But the worst of it was the betrayal by someone I had thought was my friend. I couldn't do anything about any of it. I just stood there silently, my contempt for Betty clearly etched upon my face.

"So, that's the way you want it. I don't want to hurt you, but I will." She sounded different now, older. "You did not like being with Bruce; maybe you would like a few minutes alone with Tony." She gestured to the doors of three small rooms on one side of the bay. "Take off your clothes."

Jack interrupted, "That won't be necessary. It's at Union Station."

"So, we have a marine with chivalry! And I thought you

might have liked to watch. Ah! Tony is already disappointed. Don't worry, Tony, I'll take care of you. I'm much better anyway," she cooed.

"The locker number?" She demanded of Jack.

"Two ninety-nine," he replied resignedly.

"Lock them up!" she ordered.

They shoved us into a closet-like room and slammed its steel door closed behind us. I could hear a padlock click into place on the other side. The air inside reeked; the walls were steel. There was one small window high up on one side, but it wasn't big enough for either of us to fit through. My arms ached from holding them up behind my head for so long. I finally broke down and started to cry. Jack pulled me close and put his arms around me. He held me while I cried. I didn't even have the strength to hug him back.

Day 10 - Morning

We spent a miserable and nearly sleepless night on the concrete floor of our cell. I woke up lying on my back, looking up into a ceiling of pipes and peeling paint. I painfully rolled over onto my side. Standing up brought on another wave of pain; I was stiff all over. I was cold to the core, even though we had huddled together most of the night trying to keep warm. It was the most horrible night I have ever spent. We'd been given no food or drink, and we had been forced to use a corner of the small room to pee.

Jack was down looking under the door. I crawled over and whispered in his ear, "Can you see anything?"

"Not much. Just listening." He whispered back.

"What are we going to do?"

"We've got no choice; we've got to break out, if for no other reason than to get something to eat."

"I suppose you have a plan?" I was skeptical. I strongly doubted our chances.

He leaned in close and told me what he wanted me to do. I backed into a far corner and squatted, waiting. Waiting is hard, but I was determined.

Jack looked at me, and I must have looked a sight. "I guess I need to revise my opinions on women in combat. Betty is probably the most ruthless person I have ever had the misfortune to come into contact with."

I had to smile in spite of the situation. "I sure never thought that Betty would provide the example for a female combat soldier; but you're right – ruthless is the word. She has a plan, and nothing is going to get in her way."

Jack pondered, "You have any idea what that plan might be?"

"Not a clue, but if something occurs to me, I'll be sure and let you know."

Then we sat in silence, me in the corner and Jack at the ready.

After a while I could hear the men approaching, and Jack made his move. I marveled again at his agility. He amazed me with his graceful prowess. But he had to have been even more uncomfortable than I was.

Keys rattled as the padlock jiggled. The metal door amplified it all, loudly announcing the guards' arrival. When the door swung open, I held my hand up to block the light from my eyes. I could just make out the shape of Tony.

"What the hell?" he muttered, as his eyes adjusted to the dark of the room where I squatted. "Where's the guy?" he rumbled, but he was not so foolish as to come in directly.

"I don't know!" I replied. "I woke up and he was gone. He must have gone out the window." I did my best to sound convincing.

Tony said something in another language, then switched back into English and said, "Son of a Bitch!" He came through the door looking up at the window and cussing. "Shit, Shit, Shit…."

Everything seemed to move in slow motion. Tony looked up briefly. Jack was directly above the door on top of the pipes. I didn't dare look up. As Tony cleared the doorway coming toward me, Jack sprang into action. In one smooth motion he swung down behind Tony and out through the door, catching the second man in the chest with his feet.

Tony turned to help his buddy. I could see that he was reaching under his coat for something. I knew it had to be a gun. I didn't know what else to do, so I lunged at the back of his legs hitting him just behind his knees. I bit down as hard as I could on his leg. He screamed in that other language of his, then swung his fist down hard and hit me.

When I came to, Jack was looking down at me. He looked worried. "You okay, Princess?" When I didn't answer, he spoke again. "Pam, your eyes are open. Say something."

"I'm okay." My words sounded hollow and slow.

"You shit too and fall back in it!"

"I what? You don't mean..?" I was so confused.

"No, no, no, don't worry," Jack interrupted smiling, "that's just a saying we have in the corps, but I told you to stay clear. You're going to have a nice shiner."

I reached up and touched the side of my face. I winced in pain. I looked around; we were still in the warehouse. "Where are they?" I asked nervously.

"Don't worry; they can't hurt you now."

"But, where are they?"

"Locked in the same room that we were in."

"How? What happened to them?"

"Like I told you, they can never hurt you again."

"You killed them?" I couldn't believe it was possible. He must have read the shock on my face.

He sighed, "Get a grip, girl. – It was them or us! You didn't think they were going to turn us loose, did you?"

My emotions were roiling. They were bad men, but they

were human beings. If they were dead, I was partially responsible for their deaths! It took me a few moment's reasoning to realize that Jack was right. He'd had no choice. "No, I guess not," I answered honestly. "You're right. They weren't going to let us go."

Jack scooped me up in his arms like a doll. "Let's get you to a hospital."

He carried me to our old Ford and put me in the passenger seat. I was numb for a few minutes before it all came rushing back at me; all that had happened in the past few days. What the hell was I doing here? How had I become involved? This wasn't a grand adventure, or a love story; people were dying! And the biggest question of all was: Why? What the hell were they dying for?

Day 10 - Afternoon

I don't remember much of the ride to the hospital. I vaguely remember crying, then unreasonably laughing at the absurdity of it all. Once at the hospital, Jack called the police, then dutifully sat at my side as we filled out all the paperwork and waited to see a doctor. He went with me to x-ray and the examination room. We didn't talk much. It was all routine and to be endured. Somewhere along the way he found vending machines with an endless supply of candy, cookies, sodas, and very stale sandwiches. It all tasted great. I think I ate continuously during the hours of waiting.

Finally, a doctor came in. He kicked Jack out and began my examination. When he finished, he held up x-rays of my face and told me how lucky I was; no fractures, just soft tissue damage. It all seemed pretty impersonal. After all, if they were really concerned about a person's comfort and well being, they would certainly never give a woman a gown that left her butt hanging out. He gave me a prescription for pain, and I got dressed to leave.

When I came out, Jack was talking with the detectives. "I don't understand," Jack was saying, "When we left, they were locked in that little room."

"Well, they're not there now. Whoever is behind all this is good. We could tell by tracks on the floor that there had been recent activity, but everything is gone. No bus, no table or chairs, no phone, no nothing. I've got two guys down there right now dusting for prints."

I burrowed into the conversation, "What do you mean, nothing? There should be two dead guys…"

The detective cut me off, "Well, there aren't. I talked to the guy that owns the building, and it's been empty for six years. He retired and closed the factory, and as far as he knows, no power or phone lines have been hooked up. He sure hadn't authorized anyone to use the building."

Jack asked, "Then, how did they have a phone?"

"Must have bootlegged it in somehow. That would be my guess," the detective mused.

"Guess we had better find Betty." Jack stated.

"No!" The detective was adamant. "This case has enough jokers in it. Just let us handle it." He turned to me and said, "I checked with your school, Miss, and most of the kids that came here on your bus are back at school. Apparently, they had to buy bus tickets when your bus disappeared. So at least we're not dealing with a bus load of missing kids. Another odd thing," he continued, "your school has no record of your friend Betty."

Day 10 - Evening

When we got back to our hotel room, Jack went straight to the closet and pulled out his green duffel bag and his hanging garment bag. He opened the dresser drawers and started packing neat stacks of clothing into the olive-green duffel.

"Are we going somewhere?" I asked.

"You bet. You heard Betty; she searched this place after we left yesterday."

With all that had happened I'd forgotten that little fact. I shuddered involuntarily. "Do you have room for me to put a few things in?"

He rooted around in his duffel and pulled out a small white bag. "Here, you can use my laundry bag, and we'll put your dresses in with my dress blues."

Five minutes later we were ready to leave. Jack easily slung his heavy bag over his shoulder, and we went to check out. In the car, he explained that he had already made a reservation for us at a new hotel called the Watergate.

He looked around. "Did you see anyone watching us?"

"No," I whispered as I scanned the area again.

We drove aimlessly through the city, first in one direction, then in another. After a while we drove through a residential neighborhood for a couple of blocks and pulled over and turned off our headlights. We waited silently in the dark for long minutes. I reached over, took Jack's hand in mine, and slid close to him. Just touching him helped. I was still very shaken up, but just holding his hand steadied me.

"So, who is Jack?" I desperately needed to talk about something safe and normal. "I like what I see so far, but I want to know more. We've talked about war and the marines, but who is Jack?"

"Jack is just a guy who happens to be a marine."

He paused as lights flashed at the end of the street. We watched as they moved away from us and out of sight.

"Let's see... I believe in the United States and the marines. I like dogs and cherry pie. I love our national pastime of baseball, but I'm strongly opposed to Astroturf."

"And...?" I prompted him.

He thought a moment before continuing. "I believe in capitalism, and I hate communism with every fiber of my body. I supported President Kennedy's lowering of taxes to stimulate the economy, and I oppose taxation in general. I believe in individual freedoms and oppose laws that exert unnecessary control. Hell, the ways things are going, someone will even to try to ban smoking one of these days!"

"How do you feel about religion?" I asked.

"I believe in God," he answered firmly, "but I don't particularly like churches." He turned to face me and smiled. "Most importantly, I believe in family. Family and children should be cherished. I believe in kisses. Kisses should be slow and often." He leaned over and demonstrated.

Day 11 - Morning

We checked into the Watergate Hotel the night before, and we got some much needed rest. In the morning I woke up before Jack, showered, and went out onto our small balcony. The view from our room was spectacular. Beyond the broad streets below, I could see where the Anacosta and Potomac rivers joined. The Jefferson Memorial was visible beyond the top of the Lincoln Memorial, and I knew the White House and Washington Monument were around the side of the hotel, just out of sight.

I watched planes taking off from National Airport. It had been the main airport in Washington before the larger Dulles Airport had opened a few years ago. I tried to clear my mind of the clutter of events. Too much had happened, and in so short a time. Betty had to have retrieved the explosives by now, so I knew something, or someone, was going to be blown up, and soon! All that was happening was obviously about more than protesting the war. Had the protesting been just a cover? Bruce had to have been involved at some level, and it had gotten him killed.

I let my thoughts just drift. It's amazing how things can become clearer when one shakes off preconceived beliefs, but I still couldn't figure how Jack and I fit into it all. Jack had suggested that most war protesters were just dupes, which had irritated me, but had also planted the seeds of suspicion in my mind. Had my school's organized protest trip been part of a smoke-screen for some other plan from the very beginning? Jack saw most war protestors as being just plain ignorant of the value of democracy, or as actual communist sympathizers. He said we had to be tough enough to hold the enemy at bay, or be ready to kill them to defend our freedom. Thinking about his words, I had a frightening thought: Were the protests being used as a cover up for an attack on our country? The insight was blinding! Was I thinking clearly, or just seeing bogeymen after our experience at the warehouse? The more I thought about it, the surer I was that this was a possible explanation.

My reverie was interrupted when Jack opened the curtains and popped out onto the balcony.

"Good morning." He leaned over and kissed me lightly on the cheek. "I see you've found a place of solitude."

Even though my mood was dark, I forced a smile for him. He looked so delicious in the morning sun, and I wanted to put all my fears away and just be with him. But I knew I couldn't put it off, so I decided to throw my idea out there and hope it wouldn't sound stupid.

"I've been thinking," I began, "there is something very sinister at work. Bruce wouldn't have been killed without a reason, so I'm trying to figure out what's worth killing for."

"Money. Or something worth a lot of money," Jack offered.

"That's not really what I mean. What do you kill for as a marine?" I asked.

"To protect my country." He paused, considering my question, and then he asked, "Do you think we're dealing with some sort of fifth element, or a bunch of spies? That's pretty far out there!"

"I believe there is a grander scheme afoot, Doctor Watson."

Jack rubbed his chin. "Could be. Nothing else makes sense."

I was on a roll now, so I plowed ahead, "Look, I don't think Betty or her goon friends are American. Think about it. Those guys acted like gangsters right out of some old Jimmy Cagney film. But, when they got excited, they slipped up and spoke some language that I didn't recognize. Did you?"

"No. I know some Vietnamese and a few words in Spanish, but languages are not my forte."

"So, should we go to the police and see what they think?" I asked hopefully. I was reassured that Jack seemed to be seriously considering what I'd said.

"Do you think they would really listen to us?"

"Probably not." I was crestfallen.

"We need more evidence. Something concrete that will make them sit up and pay attention."

"I agree." I was feeling better about my idea all the time. "I know it's really just a hunch, but I think it's a good one. However, I haven't got a clue about how to get real evidence."

Jack shrugged. "Maybe we should go back to the house that we followed them to."

I certainly didn't care for that idea. "Don't you think they might be there?"

Jack made grimace before replying, "Not really. More likely we'd find an empty house."

I just couldn't help teasing, "Maybe we'll find the magic matchbook."

"The magic matchbook?" Jack was puzzled.

"Sure, like in the old PI movies. You did watch old

private eye movies? Philip Marlow always finds a matchbook with the name of a hotel or restaurant, and it's a clue which leads him right to the killer."

"You'd better hope we don't find a killer, 'cause I ain't Philip Marlow. I'm just a marine."

Day 11 - Afternoon

Once we decided to check out that house again, we didn't waste time. It was a shorter drive from the new hotel. Jack parked on the next street over, and we walked through the alley and came up to it from behind. There were two doors on the back of the house: one led into the kitchen and the other led down the stairs to the basement. Both were locked. The windows were also locked, but we peered through them and saw no signs of activity. The windows on the side of the house were too high to look into, so Jack gave me a boost. Looking in at the stark room, I commented to Jack, "They're not living too well."

Jack shrugged and pointed around front. "I'll go and check the front door."

As he went out of sight, I returned to the kitchen's back door. The top of it was made up of neat little square glass panes. Suddenly I had a wild impulse. I don't know what possessed me, but I picked up a rock from the garden by the porch. With two quick blows I broke out the little windowpane nearest the handle. It was easy to reach in, open the door, and let myself inside. The first thing I noticed was that the kitchen was musty. I picked up the broken glass and dropped the pieces in the trash can.

"What the hell?" Jack's voice dripped with disapproval.

"I found it like that," I said innocently, though I knew

he'd seen the glass in my hand. "We must have missed it the first time."

"Yeah. Right!"

"Since we're in, let's check it out," I reasoned.

I opened the refrigerator. It was cold, but the offerings were sparse: a partial loaf of bread, some salami, and a six-pack of beer. It was filthy, too. I wouldn't have eaten anything in there. The cupboards were not much better: some crackers and a few chipped dishes. The glasses were old jelly jars. We worked our way systematically through the house. There was very little in the way of furniture, just a couple of chairs and a card table in the living room. Only one bedroom had a bed, and it was supported by coffee cans. The sheets were folded on the foot of the bed.

"Doesn't look very plush," I observed.

"That could be the bed I had as a boy."

What a sad thought, picturing Jack in a bed like that. There was a coating of dust everywhere in the house except for the bathroom and kitchen. We ended up back in the kitchen, coming around to it by another door from the hall. The only door left was the one to the basement. I opened the door and flipped the light switch on the wall. A single dim bulb illuminated the stairs. I went down the stairs; why I went first, I don't know. Just as I reached the bottom, I was shoved hard, and I went down.

Bam! Bam! Shots rang out. I think I screamed, and everything got confused. When I came to, which had to have been only moments later, I found myself lying face down in muck. Strong hands seized my arms and tightly bound my hands. A gag was shoved into my mouth.

I was jerked to my feet, then pushed and half-dragged up the stairs. In the daylight of the kitchen, my vision began to clear. I was looking into the face of the big-nosed man. I shuddered. He looked even more unappealing up close. He was downright frightening!

Betty came up behind me. "Did you get him?" She asked my captor.

"Nah." The man moved carefully, holding his pistol at the ready. He stood shielded from the outside by the doorframe, then he quickly moved to the wall between the windows.

He called out to Jack, "I know you're out there. If you shoot, or come around here again, I'll kill the girl. If you leave and disappear, I'll let her go."

Jack called back from the distance, "How do I know you'll keep your word?"

"You don't. But I got no reason to kill her. You two are just a nuisance. By tomorrow afternoon we'll be finished and gone. I'll leave her for you. We'll be watching the front, and if you don't drive off nice and slow past the house, I'll kill her and take my chances with you."

"Okay," Jack agreed, but I could tell that he was angry. "Guess I don't have a choice."

"That's right, you don't. We'll be watching the street. You've got two minutes."

"But remember, if you do kill her," Jack's words sounded deadly, "I'll make it my life's work to hunt you down. If you're the pro I figure you are, you don't need that kind of complication. You won't want to be looking over your shoulder from now on."

"You now only have one minute. Don't waste any more time with threats. If I am a pro, as you say, next time I'll finish you.

"So long," Jack called out, and my heart sank.

Betty pushed me down into one of the rickety kitchen chairs. She passed a rope around my chest and then pushed it under my breasts before she tightened it. She leaned over and whispered in my ear, "Don't get any bright ideas. He will gladly kill you and give it no more thought than stepping on a roach."

She left me alone with him. Wild thoughts ran through my mind. Right then, more than anything, I wanted to be back home in Illinois, or even better, with Jack. I wanted Jack's safe arms around me, reassuring me that everything was going to be all right.

Big-Nose just looked at me. His look was evil. I felt naked. When we had been held at the warehouse, I was confused; I hadn't understood what was going on. But now I knew my life was in danger, and I truly understood what it meant to be 'scared shitless'! Sweat poured from every part of my body, and I felt sick.

Betty called from the living room, "He's gone. That son of a bitch waved at me!"

Big-Nose called back, "Let's go before he changes his mind and decides to be a hero."

Betty came in and loosened the rope around me, slipping it up and around my neck. She jerked it tight, then loosened it, saying, "You yell, and he will not need a bullet."

I saw him pull a large folding knife from his pocket, and he looked very comfortable with it. "I won't shoot you, girl–it's too noisy. But I'll carve you into so many pieces that your own mother won't be able to identify your body." He paused to let his words sink in. "Understand?"

I could only nod my head.

He pulled the gag out of my mouth and laid the cold steel of the knife against my cheek. "Say it!"

I could only croak weakly, "I Understand." He shoved the gag roughly back into place.

He took my arm and led me, while Betty followed along behind me holding the rope looped around my neck. We went out the door, across the yard, and into the garage. The brown Rambler was there. We had to walk sidewise between the wall and the car, and they kept me between them. He opened the trunk. "Get in," he ordered.

I was terrified! It was difficult to get my leg up high enough to climb in with my hands tied behind me, but I managed. I was trying to figure how to fold my head in when four hands grabbed me roughly from behind and shoved me into the trunk. Momentary pain shot through me as my shin was scraped during the rough entry. Betty checked the binding on my wrists and then tied my legs together as well. Before closing the trunk, she checked the gag, too. Then she slammed the lid, and I was cast into darkness. I could hear them talking but could not make out their words. I heard the garage door open, and the car started out on what seemed to be an endless trip.

In the dark, with my painful shin, and the spare tire pressed into my back, the ride was more than miserable. The spare tire was rubbing my back raw. Things got even worse when fumes from the engine began filling the trunk. With the gag in place, I had to fight for breath, only to breathe in the foul air. Only later did I think about carbon monoxide. We finally stopped; it was a relief from the torment.

The trunk opened into another garage. They looked down at me but made no effort to get me out. I was left there a long time. I wasn't going anywhere, and they knew it. The hook-nosed man reappeared and glared down at me. He reached in and roughly heaved me out, dropping me hard onto the floor. He used his knife to cut the bindings on my legs, and then he jerked me up onto my feet. I could not walk, and my feet tingled painfully as the circulation returned. It wasn't just that my legs had been so tightly bound; it was also that I'd been in such a cramped position for so long. He was forced to half carry me into a house I'd never seen before. There was no chance of my being seen, because this was a newer house with an attached garage.

Once inside I was shoved into a closet, and the door was slammed shut. I was still standing there in the dark when Betty opened the door. She motioned for me to turn around. The removal of the bindings on my wrists brought on a new wave of pain and tingling. Finally, she pulled out the gag.

The rope was still around my neck. Betty tugged on it. She hissed loudly, leaving spittle on my face, "You make any noise and I'll leave this rope tight, with you on your tiptoes!"

Betty stepped back and picked up a sack and two cans. She tossed them into the closet. It was a McDonald's bag and two cans of Coke. I almost laughed; they were going to shoot me, stab me, and hang me, but they weren't going to starve me. Not that I wasn't grateful. I even decided not to mention that I wasn't all that fond of the fifteen-cent hamburgers.

With the door shut it was mostly dark. A string was in my face, so I pulled on it. A dull light came on. It must have been a 15 or 25 watt bulb. It wasn't bright, but I was elated. I was in a coat closet. Clothing was hung there, and things were stored on the shelf above. The clutter on the floor included a leather bag. I kicked at it. It did not move, but I hurt my foot. The bag contained a bowling ball.

I could feel the tears of fear streaming down my face.

Day 12 - Morning

I must have fallen asleep in my closet prison. I woke when the door was opened. Betty stood there with a malevolent smile on her face. I had removed the rope from around my neck, but Betty picked it up and slipped it back over my head, cinching it tightly around my neck

"Come," she ordered gruffly.

I stood shakily, and she led me into the bathroom. While I used the toilet, she stood next to me primping in the mirror. I realized that she was trying to humiliate me. I decided right then that I was not at all shy. After all, I had changed clothes and used the facilities in gym class for years. I wanted her to know that I wasn't so easily intimidated, so I decided to take a chance.

"So what happened to the two men in the warehouse?" I queried.

She turned and looked at me as I sat on the toilet. "I'll bet your marine thought he was very smart leaving that mess. I figured that you two would be pretty embarrassed when you came back with the cops and found nothing. I was hoping they'd think you two were kooks and threaten to arrest you for a false report."

"Yes, they threatened to arrest us." I lied, hoping to keep her talking.

"Good. It took both of us almost two hours to dig a hole deep enough to bury those two fools."

I tried not to imagine that scene and concentrated on getting her to tell me more. "How did you get rid of the bus?"

"Easy, I parked it back down by the protesters."

"What about Bruce? Why did you get rid of him?"

"Figured that out did you?" She merely looked amused.

"Well, Bruce was driving the bus, and then you had the bus in the warehouse. Two and two…" I tried to sound far more casual than I felt.

I didn't really expect her to tell me more, but she was too smug and proud of herself to deny me. "Well, Bruce had become a liability. He was all talk and no action. Since he got cold feet, he needed a cold swim." Her look was even more insidious than her words. I questioned how I could have been so foolish as to think Betty had ever really been my friend.

Betty continued, "No one will even miss him. More than likely, they will think you had something to do with Bruce's death, especially after they receive an anonymous tip. You certainly had the motive."

Her words made me feel as though she were standing on my grave. I had a sinking feeling that she was right.

"Moreover, the cops are certainly not going to investigate the deaths of two men when there are no bodies to prove they ever existed."

I was led by the rope back to the closet. Two bottles of water and some plain toast had been placed inside for me.

I sat down cross-legged and tried to open the bottles. It was that fancy new carbonated mineral water with a green label. The night before, the cans of Coke had had the new easy pull-tabs, but these bottles required an old-fashioned bottle-opener. I was terribly thirsty, so I risked knocking softly on the door.

"You were told to keep quiet," Betty's icy voice warned.

"I can't open the bottles."

Two Weeks

I was answered by silence. Just as I was thinking about knocking again, the door opened and Betty jerked the bottles from my hands. She opened them and unceremoniously thrust the bottles back at me, then shut the door in my face. The water was awful! I swore then and there never to drink that stuff again. After I'd eaten, I just sat there wondering what would happen next.

After a while I heard voices, and judging by the inflections in their voices, they were arguing. I got down and put my ear near the opening at the bottom of the door.

"The package is no good without the detonators." Hawk-Nose's voice now carried a definite accent, but it was not the same accent that Betty or the other men had. He must have worked hard to hide his accent.

"All right! You'll have your detonators."

"You go now!" He was nearly shouting.

"All right!" Betty sounded angry too.

I could hear her shoes clicking away across the floor, then she stopped and spoke. Her tone was now one of admiration, "Wow! Now that is a gun!"

He replied in another language. She admonished him immediately, "English, only English, remember."

He replied again with pride, "Yes this is a beauty! With this scope I can hit a target at a thousand meters."

"You had better. It's been a lot of trouble getting you in position to do this job."

His reply was confusing to me at first.

"I still don't understand how you can have someone all ready to confess to this shooting."

"Don't worry," Betty said. "The man is disturbed, and like the others, he has been carefully prepared. I probably should not tell you this, but we aren't the only ones preparing to take out key targets. Just think what the blacks would do if, say, someone like their Martin Luther King Jr., were killed. However, your target is the primary one. Just think of the disruption this will cause."

"Do not fear; I do not miss. That is why I was sent. A tall man in a big white hat is an easy target. Their president will be a great kill."

"Another trophy for your wall?"

"Of course."

I listened as Betty walked past the closet again. "I will be back soon with your detonators," she told Big-Nose. I heard the door close as Betty left the house.

I leaned back against the rear of the closet, barely able to breathe. I was living a nightmare. They were planning the unthinkable! The sickening days following President Kennedy's assassination came back to me. I was in high school, it was a Friday, and the word came in the afternoon while we were passing between periods. Just as I closed my locker, a classmate I barely knew tapped my arm and said, "Did you hear? The president has been shot."

It was such a flat statement, and it threw me into an emotional state. By the time I got to my next class, that's all anyone was talking about.

"Was he in Washington?"

"Where was he shot?"

"Why?"

Our teacher had trouble calming everyone. Just as we all began to settle down, the principal's voice came over the speakers and into our rooms. I had never heard the announcing system used, except during first period to say the 'Pledge of Allegiance' and to make daily announcements. "May I have everyone's attention?" I could visualize the old wisp of a man as he spoke in a clear voice, "The President of the United States has been shot, and he is dead. May God bless him, his family, and the United States. School is dismissed."

There were still hours before school should let out, but who could think about simple school work when we had just lost our president?

I walked home alone and found my mother glued to the TV. My father arrived home early, too. We watched the continual coverage for the next few days. I watched an actual murder, along with millions of other viewers, when Jack Ruby shot Lee Harvey Oswald on live TV. But what made the deepest impression on me was the personal grief, and strength, of the Kennedy family. It was all summed up in one image that captured the nation: a picture of three-year-old John Jr. saluting his father's casket. Tears ran down my face as I remembered again.

But it was different this time. For one thing, I might have a chance to do something to stop it. Another thing: It was personal this time. I had met President Johnson and Lady Bird. They had two lovely daughters and they were going to be grandparents soon. I had to do something to keep this from happening to our nation again. But what could I do? I was just one small person, and I was locked in a closet.

W. H. Short

I knew I couldn't afford to waste time and energy on fear and anger. I had to act fast, but how to begin? I looked around the dim closet. There wasn't much to work with: just some newspaper and a bowling ball in its bag on the floor of the closet. On the shelf above me were games: Monopoly, Clue, Password, Yahtzee, dominos, a deck of cards, and Risk (God, how I hate Risk).

Suddenly I had a thought. It was pretty crazy, but as I said, I didn't have much to work with. I opened the Yahtzee box, and sure enough, there were pencils and a score pad in the box. I used a pencil and the back of a score sheet to write a note. I wrote everything I had heard about the gun and what I knew of their plan. In fact, I wrote several notes, just to be sure. I took off my jacket and placed one of the notes in its pocket. I put the others in my pants pocket. If the opportunity came, I was ready to plant the other notes. I knew that if I left my jacket behind, Jack would somehow find this closet and my note.

I took the bowling ball out of its bag and tried hefting it. It was heavy! I put it back in its bag and tried again, lifting it by the handles. It was much easier to lift that way. I was going to be ready when Betty came back.

Hours passed and no one came. My back hurt, and I began to wonder if maybe they were planning to just leave me there. Then someone was there, unlocking the door. I poised myself, ready to spring. When the door opened, I swung the heavy bowling ball bag with all my might. It was Big-Nose. He ducked beneath the arc of the bag as it sailed over the top of him. I hadn't let go of the handles, so I followed the bag as it continued on out into the small hallway. When I turned around, he smiled at me for the first time, and then his fist exploded into my face.

Day 12 - Afternoon

When I came to, I was lying in the sun on a hot roof. Its rocky surface was burning into my arms and legs. But what hurt the most was that my arms and legs were tightly bound together with gray tape. I struggled, but to no avail. I could not call out, and breathing was difficult because a foul tasting rag had been forced into my mouth, and tape had been wrapped all the way around my head to hold the gag in place. It tasted like a dirty sock. It turns out that's just what it was.

I felt like crying, but realized that if I did, I might suffocate. So I concentrated on how mad I was. Someone had told me that people who are angry don't cry. I tried to crawl or scoot, and I made some slow progress at first, but I couldn't get far. When I looked back I could see that I was tied, like a dog, to a pipe sticking out of the roof. It seemed like I was there for hours, baking in the hot sun. My thirst was all consuming. I fought off feelings of hopelessness. Now and then clouds passed over, providing occasional relief as the afternoon progressed. After what seemed an eternity, the sun began dipping down toward the horizon, and it started getting cooler. Unexpectedly, a shadow crossed over me. I knew it had to be the big-nosed man or Betty. I kept my eyes closed. I heard the sound of steel being drawn against steel. I reflexively opened my eyes and breathed a sigh of relief. Jack was standing over me.

What I had heard was the sound of Jack drawing his K-Bar combat knife from its sheath. Jack used it to slash the tape on my arms. I knew the knife was razor sharp; I had watched

144

him sharpen it one evening. He leaned down and placed his finger to his lips, "Shhh…"

He worked to remove my gag. He cut the tape and pulled it away, pulling my hair at the same time. It hurt, but I kept quiet. He slashed the tape on my legs, laid down his knife, and drew me to him. I hugged him fiercely, almost insensible with the relief of seeing him again.

Jack's voice was coarse when he whispered in my ear, "That bastard is up here somewhere. Have you seen him?"

"No." What little voice I had was lost in the wind.

"Go down the stairs and call the cops." He pushed a business card into my hand. It was Detective Thomas' card.

"Where are we? How did you find me?" I whispered gratefully.

"Just got lucky." Jack pulled the remaining tape off of me. "I want you to get off this roof. We're twenty stories up. That door over there leads to the stairs. Just run down and call Thomas. He'll send the cavalry."

I held tightly to Jack's shirt. "Come with me," I pleaded.

"I have to find him," he whispered. I reluctantly released my hold.

I could not move very fast; my legs felt so heavy. I managed to stumble to the door of the roof. I looked back at Jack, but he was already gone. He was a man on a mission.

I opened the door to find Betty standing there. She was very surprised to see me.

"What the hell?" She stepped back and was reaching for something in her jacket.

I still don't know where I found the reserve of strength. Maybe it was my resolve not to be captured and tied up again, or maybe it was the terror I felt at what Betty and Hawk-Nose were trying to do. It was probably a combination of both. Her hand reappeared holding a pistol. I jumped onto her, which sent the gun flying. She punched me in the face and was on top of me as we went down together. I could not reach to punch her back, so I used what I had: my head. I hit her full in the face with a head-butt. I must have gotten her good, because blood splattered everywhere. We fought, punching and gouging at each other. A square metal object flew from her pocket. I managed to kick it out of her reach.

She was a better fighter than I, but she was hampered by the narrow space of the stairwell. She hit me hard on my left breast, and the pain jolted me. I drilled her right back, using all my strength, and made a direct hit on her right breast. She cried out in pain, giving me time to get to my feet. I knew I could not go on much longer. She tried to retrieve the metal box, and that distracted her long enough to give me time to jump over her. I tried to get down the stairs, but she grabbed my pant leg and held on, causing me to fall belly down, sliding to the landing below. The stairs were metal, and they scraped and cut me as I fell. Betty landed on top of me and got her arm around my neck. Before she could clamp it down, I ducked my head and bit down hard on her arm. She screamed in pain. I rolled over, my back to the wall, laboring to get breath back into my battered body. Moments later, she stood over me holding her bloody arm.

"You bitch!" She screamed. "You fucking bitch!"

I kicked at her with both feet, launching her down the next

section of stairs. I stood and looked down after her, determined to finish this. But there was no need. Her head was at an odd angle, and her eyes were empty. The fall must have broken her neck.

I just stood there, staring. I knew right then that the sight would always haunt me. I wanted to turn away, but I had caused her death, so I forced myself to look. Long moments passed as I fought, gasping, to get air back into my lungs. I picked up the little metal box. It looked like a transistor radio, antenna and all. There was a simple switch on the top which was taped in the off position. I realized this must be the transmitter to set off the bomb on the bus.

Then I heard it! The sound ripped through my gut. The definite sound of a rifle being fired.

My heart wrenched with the feeling that President Johnson must be dead. I'm not sure what drove me, but I went back up the stairs. I picked up Betty's gun and went out onto the roof. I moved toward the noise. I peeked around a large air conditioning unit and could see two men fighting. Both were covered in blood, probably from rolling around on the rocky surface. Hawk-Nose had Jack down and was choking him. I walked two steps forward and fired at his back. I missed.

I nearly dropped the gun in my reaction to firing it. I had seen guns fired on TV and in movies, but I had not anticipated the magnitude of the noise or the gun's jumping kick of power. I looked down – I couldn't believe I had missed! Jack was on top now, and they were fighting furiously. It was a sight watching two men trying to kill one another. Suddenly Jack gained the upper hand. He had Hawk-Nose's head and was beating him senseless against the hard edge of the roof. I was frozen in place. Finally, Jack stood up and walked over to me.

"The president..?" My voice was hoarse and strained, filled with fear of the inevitable.

"He's fine."

He took the gun from my hands. I watched as Jack calmly walked over and shot the unconscious man twice. He dropped the gun and came back to me.

Suddenly, the roof was alive with men. I wanted to hug Jack but I couldn't.

Day Thirteen - Evening

Twenty-four hours had passed since the chaos on the roof had ended. I'd been kept in the hospital overnight for observation. I probably could have insisted on going back to the hotel with Jack, but I just couldn't be with him right now.

I had not slept very well. I learned that it's hard to get much rest in a hospital. The nurses kept waking me up just as I would manage to get into a restful sleep. There always seemed to be something they needed to do. So I had slept and awoken several times, not just because of the nursing staff, but also because my mind was alive with confusing thoughts.

I finally fell into a sound sleep as dawn was approaching. I had made my decision, and I was not happy about it.

When I awoke in the bright sunlight of morning, Jack was standing at the foot of the bed looking at me. Two other men were there also: a man in an expensive suit, and Detective Thomas. All three wore grave expressions of concern.

"So, do I look that bad?"

Jack gave me one of his glorious smiles. "On the contrary, my dear, you look wonderful."

"Miss Marks," the man in the suit was speaking, "I'm Special Agent Walt with the Secret Service." He walked to my bedside and showed me his badge and ID. I studied them carefully, and then smiled at him. I was relieved to know the Secret Service was finally involved.

He spoke in a soft, well educated tone, "I want to thank you on behalf of a grateful country. You and Staff Sergeant Jakes have prevented a terrible thing. President Johnson sends you his personal thanks."

Little waves of conflicting emotions and thoughts passed through me. "I'm sorry if I don't seem very grateful right now. The whole episode has been very traumatizing."

Agent Walt nodded in agreement. "I can understand and appreciate your position. I'm sure you'd like some explanations, too. I am also hoping that you can answer some important questions for me."

"Well, you do know that Betty and Hook-Nose killed Bruce, don't you? And that they buried those two men we left behind in the warehouse?" I asked.

Detective Thomas grinned, "Well I guess that closes that case."

Agent Walt nodded. "Yes, and we believe the woman you knew as Betty was a Soviet agent, one Katrina Voling. She came into the country on a student visa as Gloria Winsted, from England, and disappeared. We do not yet know who the man was."

I looked at Jack. "So, how did you find me?"

"When I drove down the street away from the house where you were kidnapped, Detective Thomas here was waiting at the end of the block. He'd followed us from the hotel, but had lost us. After I explained that they were holding you, he had me jump in his car, and we swung around and watched the house. When the Rambler left, we followed it to the house in Maryland where they held you until the assassination attempt. It took a while to coordinate the forces of the DC police, FBI, and Maryland state and local police. We really didn't know what we were dealing with yet. The FBI tapped their phone, but that didn't do any good. They were smart and stayed off the phone. But we were ready when they left the next day. The only problem was that we didn't realize that they had taken you along with them."

Jack had a paper sack from which he produced my jacket. "When they left, I broke in, hoping to find you. But all I found was the note you left in your jacket. Once we knew it was a conspiracy to kill the president, we called in the Secret Service."

"So, what happened to all the other kids from my school?" I asked.

Detective Thomas answered, "We believe that Bruce just drove off with the bus while they were out protesting. We have spent the better part of the day on the phone with your school, and with the parents of your fellow protestors, and we've been able to account for all of them."

I was relieved, but I had more questions. "Why did they kill Bruce, and why chase us around? Why were we involved?"

Detective Thomas was ready. "That's complicated, and the best we can come up with is that once all the other students had gone home, that left just you. They wanted you to go home too, so they tried to scare you off. The problem was that you and Jack didn't scare so easily. As you know, Bruce was a ladies' man, and we've learned he was sleeping with a girl on the White House staff. She told Bruce the president's schedule, and he must have passed that information along to Betty. We believe he was an American communist who may have gotten cold feet when he found out that the actual mission was to kill the president.

"That makes sense," I added. "Betty told me Bruce was

long on talk and short on action. But I still don't understand how their plan was supposed to work."

"It was really a very good plan, and it might have worked if you and Jack had not interfered. The man you refer to as Hawk-Nose must have been a very good shot if he was going to shoot from a range of over 900 yards. That distance is beyond the range the Secret Service had previously considered the boundary of effective shooting. Of course, in the future we will expand that boundary. After the shooting, we believe the plan was to blow up the bus down near the picket lines as a diversion. That distraction would give the shooter time to escape."

"I was so afraid up there on the roof! I thought the president had been killed."

"Don't worry; after we got your warning note, the president was never in any danger at all from those two. Once I called it in, the president's schedule was changed. We don't advertise it, but there is a Secret Service agent who bears a strong resemblance to the president from a distance, especially when he wears the big white hat and all. We usually just use him as a placeholder when practicing certain official ceremonies. After my call, Agent Jones replaced the president, and he was the man they actually saw. Agent Jones was standing behind a very clear piece of bullet proof glass. We wanted time to get this guy. Thanks to you, there was never any chance that they would succeed in killing the president. Anyway, the point is, your little note saved him."

"I'm still a little hazy on just how Jack found me on the building top."

Detective Thomas chimed in, "Your note provided us

with the range of the gun and the date of the attempt. We could figure the time of day because we knew the president's planned schedule. It was just a matter of calculating the various places where a shooter could be. We drew circles on a map and checked out the possible buildings. Jack just happened to be the one to find you. I'm sure glad you kept them from blowing up the bus. There could have been a lot of kids hurt or killed."

Jack said, "These two men just took a chance on us, Pam, and they made a maximum effort to save you. From a legal point of view, there was no hard evidence, just your note. That was really good thinking, leaving a note."

I was at a loss for words. "Thanks," was all I managed, and then I had another thought. "I'm guessing we're the big news story of the day. Are we the front page headline? Not that I'd want my father to read about me in the paper. If we are, I guess I need to call him."

Detective Thomas interjected, "There's nothing in the paper because they don't know."

"They don't know?" That seemed impossible to me.

Agent Walt handed me a piece of paper. "Would you please sign this, Miss Marks? It's a non-disclosure statement I have prepared. We don't want it to get out that there was a near miss with the president."

I took the paper and pen he offered. "Did Jack sign one of these, too?"

"Yes, and so did Detective Thomas and the two FBI agents involved."

I signed the agreement without any reservation.

"The public and press can never know, and these non-disclosure statements help to ensure that they never do." Agent Walt was in his element. "Here's the deal; this country has been through a lot in recent years, especially since President Kennedy was shot. There are thousands of threats against the President every year, and several dozen, like this one, that are actual conspiracies. However, this is the closest call we've had since the Kennedy shooting. It has been decided at the highest levels to say nothing unless it leaks out."

"So, what if it does leak out?" I inquired.

Agent Walt was reassuring. "If it does surface, we won't hide the facts. But the non-disclosure works in your favor too; as their kidnap victim, you'd really get worked over by the press. The press can be relentless. And often, with today's pressure to get first scoops, the initial story is often wrong, or at the least may contain distorted facts."

I must have looked perplexed; in fact, I was. "So, that's it?"

"Pretty much." Agent Walt shook my hand and left. Then Detective Thomas shook my hand and left another one of his cards on the table by my bed. He left, and I was alone with Jack.

I looked at Jack. He looked pretty beat up, too. He looked down at me for a long minute. Finally Jack asked, "So what are you going to do?"

"I'm going home."

"I thought that maybe we had become a couple."

"We were, and now we're not."

"So what changed?"

"I watched you shoot a man in cold blood."

"Hell, you killed Betty!"

"It was an accident."

"Cold blood or hot blood; by my count that pair committed at least five to eight capital crimes. I was determined that that SOB was never going to get his hands on you again, or ever get another opportunity to take a shot at our president. I saved the taxpayers a lot of money."

"It was not your decision to make, Jack. Decisions about life and death are left to a court in this country. That's why we have laws."

"Just so you know, it was my decision. As a marine, I'm paid by taxpayers to make life and death decisions regarding the enemies of this nation. Had either of them been a US citizen, it might have been different, but they were enemies of this country. Anyone serving in the military is obligated to make those decisions in combat. If I make the wrong decision, I might be court-martialed. If it's the right decision, I might get a medal, or be told 'well done'. But in any case, my job is to kill the enemies of this country. I am certainly obligated to protect senior officers, and be assured, no matter what my political feelings, I will protect my Commander-In-Chief!"

I hesitated before answering, "I guess we've finally found something that we agree about: the protection of the president and this country. But I am surer than ever that it must be done by the law."

"I believe there is another thing we agree about. I'm in love with you, and you're in love with me."

It was not easy, but I looked him right in the eye. "That may be, but Jack, I believe you were wrong. You should have turned him over to the cops or the Secret Service. I'm not sure I can live with the way you handled it."

Jack turned and left. It was not easy to see him leave, but right at that time, I had to let him go.

Day 14 - Morning

Detective Thomas drove me to the bus station. He had retrieved my clothes from Jack at the hotel. We rode in silence until he pulled up at the station. He turned and told me straight out, "As a police officer, I deal with people of all stripes; a lot are bad ones, but there are good ones, too. I believe that you are making the wrong decision regarding Jack. You and I both know that he cares for you very much. I think you blame Jack for allowing you to be captured a second time. Please don't let that come between you. Jack was almost crazy trying to get you back. It was all I could do to keep him from breaking into that house and taking you back by force. I've rarely seen a man so smitten."

I was taken aback by his interference. "Mr. Thomas, I appreciate what you're trying to do, but it's not that." I could not contain myself any longer; I had kept it in too long. "I killed Betty by accident; it was self defense. Jack killed Hawk-Nose after he was down and was no apparent threat."

"No, Miss Marks. We believe that the man you call Hawk-Nose was a professional killer. I received a telex from Interpol this morning. He is a man known by several names, the most prominent of which is Felix. Felix is suspected of more than forty murders. Jack must be one very tough guy to take down a man like that. No, the only way to be sure a man of that caliber cannot hurt you, is to kill him. We would have had a tough time holding him. He has escaped from six maximum security facilities that we know of."

"I cannot help the way I feel right now. It was horrible. I believe the law is the only way to deal with criminals."

"Police officers must make decisions like that from time to time, too. I'll never tell anyone what you've told me, and you should never repeat it again. I understand, but there are those, like you, who do not understand that sometimes violence is necessary to stop violence. Please reconsider and try to understand Jack. I've been told by my pastor that understanding and forgiveness are two of the highest virtues."

Now, as I ride alone on this bus going home, I can only wonder what might have been. I can't help thinking how different we were, and how different our ideals were. Yet, I was so drawn to Jack, an exciting and violent man.

No matter what happens in the future, these last two weeks have changed my life. I now know what my purpose is: I will finish school and study law. I can see now that only the law can preserve this great country. If Jack and I were to somehow get back together, I know he would support my quest for the law.

I still have a lot to work out in my mind. It will take time to process all that has taken place. I miss Jack already, and I know he is a good man. I do love him, but, for now at least, I need to get on with my life.

* * * * * * * *

December 1968

1968 was an interesting year. I fell in love, and I just had a baby boy. I named him Jack. Just after I got back from Washington, President Johnson announced that he would not run for another term. He also became a grandfather; his daughter, Lynda, had a little girl in October.

Two weeks after we left Washington, Dr. Martin Luther King Jr. was assassinated. Following his death, riots erupted in Washington D.C., Chicago, and Baltimore. Anything that might have happened as a result of the events of our story was lost in the tumultuous events that followed. In June it looked as though Senator Bobby Kennedy would win the Democratic presidential nomination, but, he too, was assassinated. He was killed on the night he won the California primary. Surprisingly, Nixon won the presidency in November.

I have been lucky enough to have been loved by someone, and to love him in return. That feels great! I love you Jack, wherever you are, and wherever you go in life. I have decided to forgive you. I am continuing to study the law, and I am hoping one day to understand you and your ideals.

As I sit writing, I have no idea where little Jack's real father is. What gives me hope for us all is that right now three astronauts are circling the moon in Apollo 8, even as the war goes on. Jack, you were right about our astronauts; they will succeed in getting to the moon. Nothing can stop this great nation as long as individual citizens are free to stop our enemies, and we continue to explore new frontiers.

* * * * * * * *

As young Jack reached the end of his mother's journal, he found six very faded photographs taped on the last few pages. There were two of Jack and Pam. Jack was in dress blues and Pam was wearing a formal gown. They were standing with President Johnson and a marine general. The other four were of Jack in civilian clothes in various areas around Washington. Below that were two yellowed newspaper clippings. The tape was so old that it, too, had yellowed, and was mostly unstuck.

The first article featured a faded picture of Pam and Jack standing with President Johnson. It was cut from the Washington Post, as indicated by the words at the top of the page. In his mother's now familiar handwriting was written: March 1968.

Hero Welcomed

The President and Mrs. Johnson gave a dinner party on Saturday night at the White House. The guest of honor was Medal of Honor recipient Marine Staff Sergeant Jackson Jakes. The President presented Staff Sergeant Jakes with the award last Monday in a Rose Garden ceremony.

Staff Sergeant Jakes won the medal for defense of Hill 811 in the 1967 battle of Kai Sun. When marine forces on the hill were overrun by NVA forces, Sergeant Jakes stood ground and held the hill after all marines in his unit were killed or wounded. He is credited with killing eighty-four enemy troops assaulting the hill. He has become known in the corps as the King of Hill 811.

Other guests included the Commandant of the Marine Corps, General Chapman Jr. and Mrs. Chapman, Secretary of Defense Dean Rusk and Mrs. Rusk, and the president's daughters.

A second article had been cut from an unknown newspaper.

Feb 23, 1969

AP Marine Staff Sergeant Jackson Jakes, winner of the Congressional Medal of Honor, was declared missing in action and presumed dead after an engagement in Ben Hoa. US troops came under attack in a well-organized pre-dawn battle for control of the USAF airfield in the area. This was one of a series of offenses by the NVA, and one of the first major battles since the bombings were halted last November by President Johnson, and President Nixon took office.

The battle began with rocket attacks against US forces. Their base was in a safe area where there had been little enemy action. US forces were badly outnumbered. Lieutenant Carl Green and Staff Sergeant Jakes led a team of marines on a counter attack to the flank as the major ground action began. The flank attack broke the enemy offensive push; however Staff Sergeant Jakes was wounded.

After the battle a helicopter retrieved all of the marines except the wounded Jakes, who stayed in the landing zone. Jakes continued to provide protection until all other wounded marines could be extracted. A corporal who witnessed the action reported seeing Jakes bleeding from wounds that appeared to be severe. Staff Sergeant Jakes was still standing and firing as we flew out of sight. Six hours later, four infantry companies of the army second corps entered the area and were unable to find Staff Sergeant Jakes.

Epilogue

November 1993

First Lieutenant Jack Campbell stepped from the car and then went around to open the door for his mother. The marine corporal on duty at the curb saluted Jack sharply. Jack returned the salute before assisting Pam from his sports car. Pam was dressed in a formal gown that was a little too tight and long to easily get in or out of a low car. They stopped briefly at the coatroom where he checked his hat and she checked her fur. Jack took her arm and led her down the long hall of the Officers' Club to the ballroom.

"So, how is Charley?" She asked idly, just to make conversation.

"He's fine. He seems to have recovered well. He went back to work last week."

"That's good."

The room was already half filled with guests. All of the tables were reserved, and Jack stopped at a table near the front of the room. Neat little place cards were by each setting. "1st Lt. J. P. Campbell" and "Her Honor P. S. Marks-Campbell".

"This must be the place," Pam commented as Jack held the chair for her.

"Would you like something to drink?" Jack asked.

"Gin and tonic."

"I'll fetch," Jack responded, "since they will probably be slow to start serving. Be right back." With that he turned and walked toward the large bar on the far side of the room.

Pam took a moment to take in the entire room. A large banner was draped across the middle of one wall. Its bold letters read: "Semper Fi – 218 Years of Marine Glory. Happy Birthday!" A huge cake dominated the center of the room. There was a speaker's podium dominating the front of the room with flags on both sides of it. A tasteful bunting of patriotic dressing was hung across the entire stage. This was the Marine Corps Birthday Ball.

Why had she allowed Jack to talk her into coming? This was a life that she had left behind years ago, a life that never really started. Even as she wondered why, she knew the answer; it was because Jack had asked her. She had not seen much of him during the past few months, and she had never really talked with him about his real father. The night she had given him her journal to read, she had gone to bed, leaving him alone. He was gone by morning, having left the journal behind with a note thanking her.

"Pam?" A familiar voice came from behind her. "Pamela Marks, is that you?"

She turned but could not answer at first. It was a ghost. "Jack?"

He was older, and probably a few pounds heavier than he had been. Lines around his eyes indicated his age. Even though his hair was cut short in the regulation fashion, she could see his temples were graying. He was wearing Chief Warrant Officer dress blues and even more ribbons than she remembered. The Medal of Honor was hanging around his neck. It was not an ostentatious display; it was just part of Jack.

She stood, and he took her hands. Instinctively, she hugged him, and then she started to cry. Finally, he held her back away from him. "Let me just look at you," he rumbled. She looked his face over in detail. He had a few new scars, but he still looked good to her.

"I thought you were dead. I read about it in the paper." She picked up her purse and pulled out a tissue, and she dabbed at her eyes. They sat down together, holding hands.

"I was wounded and spent more than eighteen months in the hospital. When I got leave afterward, I went to Carbondale and looked for you. I found out your father had died, and your mother had sold the house and moved. I went to the University of Wisconsin, and all I could find out was that you had been a student but had dropped out or transferred. I searched for you off and on for more than five years."

"Yes, I got married and transferred to the University of Illinois. Mother moved in with her sister."

"Married? Are you here with your husband?"

"No–divorced; have been for years. I'm here with my son, who is a marine too." Pam hesitated as another thought popped into her head. "Are you here with your wife?"

"Nope. Never found the right woman, or the time."

"What happened to Gunny Callahan?"

Jack grinned the same grin that she had seen so many times on young Jack. "He is retired and living in Florida. I played golf with him just last month."

"I can't believe you're still in the marines."

"Sometimes I can't believe it myself. But this is it for me. Got my thirty in; I'm no longer a marine as of the first of

December."

"I believe I remember someone telling me, 'once a marine, always a marine'."

Lieutenant Jack Campbell returned, smiling. "Well, I see you two have found each other." He handed his mother her drink, and the older Jack a beer.

Pam looked at the two together. The resemblance was startling. No one could doubt that they were father and son: The same nose, eye set, shape of the ears, and other features. It was uncanny. The uniform made her son look like the younger version of the older man. She had never realized just how much. "You arranged this!" She smilingly accused her son.

"Guilty."

"But how?"

"After I read your journal, I went to the base library and looked up Medal of Honor winners. There are not many, and there are few still on active duty. Once I realized that he was still alive, and still in the Corps, it was just a matter of locating him. It was only a little more difficult arranging for you two to sit together at this ball. It seems the commanding general is fond of you, Sir, so he was only too happy to help."

The older Jack said, "I was wondering why this shave tail Lieutenant was hanging around."

Pam knew the moment of truth had arrived. She looked at the older man. "Jack, meet Jack. And if that's not plain enough, this is your son."

"Once I saw the two of you together, I surmised as much."

Pam looked at her son and apologized. "Things are

different now, but in the sixties, a pregnant woman needed to be married. Charley knew the situation when we married, and he accepted things as they were. Charley is a good man. I know he always tried to be a good father to you. I guess Charley always hoped that love would grow between us, but it never did. I'd like to think that I really tried. After your sister was born, we just grew in different directions. Maybe…"

The younger Jack held up his hand. "Mother, you owe me no more explanations; this is enough for me."

Pam reached out and took a hand from each of them.

****

Two weeks later, Pam and Jack were married. Their son was the best man at their wedding, and he gave the bride away.

The End

"Some people spend an entire lifetime wondering if they made a difference in the world. But, the Marines don't have that problem."

Ronald Reagan

W. H. Short

Historical Note – Medal of Honor:

The Medal of Honor is a military award that came into being during the Civil War. It is the highest award for valor in action against an enemy force which can be bestowed upon an individual serving in the Armed Services of the United States. Generally the MOH is presented to its recipient by the President of the United States of America in the name of Congress, it is often called the *Congressional Medal of Honor.*

Only 3,461 Medals have been awarded over the years. There are currently 111 living recipients of the medal (For the most current information, go to www.cmohs.org. Most have been issued in war:

1,522	Civil War
426	Indian Wars
15	Korea 1871
110	Spanish American
4	Samoa
80	Philippine Insurrection
59	Boxer Rebellion
56	Mexican Campaign
8	Haiti
3	Dominican Republic
124	World War I
2	Nicaraguan Campaign
464	World War II
131	Korean War
245	Vietnam
2	Somalia
1	Iraq-Afghan
9	Unknown
193	Non-Combat

Non-Combat awards have been given to recognize accolades and deeds so vast that only the Medal of Honor will suffice.

One Medal of Honor has been issued in the current War on Terror (Iraq-Afghanistan conflict):

Two Weeks

The Medal of Honor was awarded posthumously to the family of Army Sgt. 1ˢᵗ Class Paul R. Smith on April 4, 2005 for action in Baghdad, Iraq in 2003.

Sergeant Smith led a defense of a compound next to the airport against a much larger force of elite Special Republican Guard troops, manning a heavy machine gun, repeatedly firing and reloading three times before he was mortally wounded. Fellow soldiers said his actions killed 20 to 50 Iraqis, allowed wounded American soldiers to be evacuated, and saved an aid station and perhaps 100 lives.

On 11 November, 2006, President George W. Bush announced that the Medal of Honor will be awarded posthumously to Marine Cpl. Jason Dunham. In April 2004, Dunham was leading a patrol in an Iraqi town near the Syrian border when the patrol stopped a convoy of cars leaving the scene of an attack on a marine convoy.

According to military and media accounts of the action, an occupant of one of the cars attacked Dunham and the two fought hand-to-hand. As they fought, Dunham yelled to fellow Marines, "No, no, watch his hand!" The attacker then dropped a grenade and Dunham hurled himself on top of it, using his helmet to try to blunt the force of the blast.

Dunham was critically wounded in the explosion and died eight days later at Bethesda Naval Hospital in Maryland.

President Bush spoke at the dedication of the National Museum of the Marine Corps in Virginia. "As long as we have Marines like Corporal Dunham, America will never fear for her liberty."

www.ingramcontent.com/pod-product-compliance
Lightning Source LLC
Chambersburg PA
CBHW070943200626
46811CB00025B/872

* 9 7 8 0 9 7 9 7 0 3 6 0 7 *